DEN OF DEATH

Simms and Dillinger spotted the men in trench coats, too. They were filing through the doorway, grim eyes searching the crowd, hands already reaching deep inside their pockets. Thinly veiled behind the hash smoke, they moved, swift dark silhouettes in the gloomy light.

Through the wafting smoke, Vic Gabriel made eye contact with one of the trench-coated strangers. Somehow they looked familiar to Gabriel, or perhaps he should have recognized them. Or...

"Russians!" Atlas warned.

That was all Vic Gabriel and his commandos needed to hear.

Eagle Force #4:

RED FIRESTORM

by Dan Schmidt

BANTAM BOOKS
NEW YORK · TORONTO · LONDON · SYDNEY · AUCKLAND

RED FIRESTORM

A Bantam Book / March 1990

ISBN 0-553-28373-1

Published simultaneously in the United States and Canada

Bantam Books are published by Bantam Books, a division of
Bantam Doubleday Dell Publishing Group, Inc. Its trademark,
consisting of the words "Bantam Books" and the portrayal of a
rooster, is Registered in U.S. Patent and Trademark Office and in
other countries. Marca Registrada. Bantam Books, 666 Fifth Ave-
nue, New York, New York 10103.

PRINTED IN THE UNITED STATES OF AMERICA

OPM   0 9 8 7 6 5 4 3 2 1

For Suzi, whose understanding, patience, and devotion set the storm behind.

Chapter 1

Within minutes, he knew they would be running in the shadows of death. The reassuring weight of the twin, pearl-handled Colt .45 automatics holstered beneath his tiger-striped windbreaker, Bad Zac Dillinger was grimly intent on keeping his appointment with an ugly fate. It was simply a question of who would be checking out first. And Bad Zac Dillinger wasn't ready to arrive in the Great Void yet, hell no. The former private investigator figured the long-haired guy in the sandals upstairs had racked up a pretty good card of sins on his freebooting, womanizing ways, and Dillinger didn't have the first excuse ready to hand the most famous of Jews. Not that excuses would buy him any time in purgatory, no, sir. Excuses, he knew, usually made people hammer a guy into the ground that much harder.

"Man, you sure this is such a smart thing to do? I mean, tellin' husbands their wives are head-bobbin' somewhere else is one thing, Bad One. Starin' down Mafia guns is somethin' else altogether, particularly when some godfather's broad's the one been doin' the head-bobbin'. You may be ugly as sin and hardheaded as mountain rock, Bad Zac D, but I know you gotta be catchin' my drift, 'cause you're far from stupid, man."

Dillinger unholstered one .45 automatic at a time. He drew the slides back, chambering the opening round for battle in each Blood and Guts special. Forget setting the

1

safety. Cocked but not locked, right. Bad Zac Dillinger scratched an itch somewhere in his thinning white hair and zipped his windbreaker halfway up. He was pumped with adrenaline, primed to kick ass. Blue eyes as hard as an arctic glacier, the ex-P.I. looked at Johnny Simms, as the short, stocky black ex-merc screwed the silencers on two mini-Uzis, then slapped a 32-round clip into the magazine of each Israeli 9mm Parabellum flesh-eater. Cocking the bolts on both mini-Uzis, Simms holstered the subguns in shoulder rigging beneath a brown leather flight jacket that was about two sizes too big for his five-foot-eight-inch, one-hundred-and-eighty-pound frame.

"I didn't see anybody draggin' ya here by the scruff of your black neck, Johnny Boy."

Simms cracked a grin, shook his head. "Leave it up to the ol' Bad One to get a bellyful of beer in me, then make a fifty-fifty recovery-fee proposition. Shit. This was s'posed to been just a night out on the town, me and you, talkin' over old times, rappin' about the good ole days in Central America where we both almost got wasted. I didn't expect to be mixin' it up with mob goons who I ain't got nothin' against."

"Nothin' against, huh. Tell that to Paula Jessup, Johnny. Lemme tell you something else. Two things I hate more than anything in the world. One's being used. Two's not getting paid. Manny Vitelli did both to me. Me and Manny got a big score to settle, and I'm in the mood to bring the whole joint down around the old fuck's ears."

"Yeah, Zachary, but this is an old tab that goes back six months. Why wait till tonight?"

"Because Paula Jessup floated up on the beach in Lauderdale yesterday, Johnny, that's why."

"Sorry, man. I didn't know that. It sounded like maybe this Paula Jessup was just a special someone who chipped away a little stone around that concrete heart of yours."

2

"Don't be sorry, Johnny Boy. I didn't tell ya the whole story about Paula and Manny. You see, I knew Manny was mob when he hired me to find his girlfriend. A promised ten grand got the better of my judgment at the time because I got two ex-wives and the IRS breathing fire up my ass. I found Paula, all right, getting ready to split town with some new head-bobbin' beau she'd found. I brought her back to Manny, and he was so blind pissed-off jealous he suddenly forgot he owed me that ten grand. Slapped the hell out of her right in front of me, had his goons draw iron on me when I went into my white-knight routine, and escorted me outside. They threw four Ben Franklins at my feet and told me to get lost. Now. . . there's a good reason why you wait awhile on something like this."

Simms nodded. "Time softens."

"And lowers your guard, right."

"And vengeance is sweet."

"And vengeance, Johnny Boy, is mine, sayeth one Bad Zac Dillinger. And Johnny," Dillinger said, tight-lipped, "Paula Jessup wasn't a bad kid either. She was all of nineteen, just mixed-up like any teenager. Remember that when you walk in after me. The money's not the point, really. It's a question of pride. And vengeance for a mixed-up kid who didn't deserve to get carved up like a Thanksgiving turkey. You reading me?"

"I'm right behind you, Bad One. All the way."

And there was no doubt in Dillinger's mind that Johnny Simms, a fifth-degree blackbelt, would be right there when the lead started to fly and ass needed to be kicked. They'd done hard time, yeah, in the bush down in Central America, training and later fighting beside CIA-backed contra rebels in what had been, and still is, in Dillinger's mind, a twisted, sordid affair of killing between the haves and the have-nots for control of one huge fucking mess that's the lower Americas. Seasoned warriors, blooded in the heat of all-out combat during the

Central American campaign, both Dillinger and Simms knew they could count on each other's lethal martial skills. More importantly, though, they were both men who could rely on the bond of loyalty that existed between them. Loyalty that had been earned through blood and fire, sweat and sacrifice.

The parking lot was packed with cars around the stone-and-glass facade of the Babylon III. Rock music blared from the marbled foyer as two beefy bouncers in black tuxedos opened the mahogany doors to let patrons in and out of the strip joint. Manny Vitelli owned the strip joint, one of six new Babylons he'd recently opened up in Miami and Fort Lauderdale. Vitelli, Dillinger had discovered during the past few months, had other interests outside of the porn racket. The mafioso dabbled in cocaine traffic, prostitution, and contract killing, too. Standard trade for any Mafia kingpin, sure. Only Dillinger had done the mob boss a favor, and the ex-P.I. had wrestled with his conscience the whole time since for stepping over onto the other side of the tracks. The guilt feelings had bitten even deeper during the past day, gnawing at his guts like a cancer—because he felt responsible in some way for the death of Paula Jessup. There must be honor even among thieves and assassins, Dillinger believed. There is even some code of honor among vipers like Vitelli and his cutthroats. There was definitely a code of honor that Dillinger believed in living by, no matter who or what he dealt with. Okay, Dillinger had played by their rules, expected them to at least humor him with their own code of honor, and had gotten burned in the process. Honor aside, he was intent on doing more than just sweeping clean Manny's house of filth. A lot more. Like burn clean. Burn to the ground. Purge by hellfire. It was going to be quite a night in Miami, Dillinger suspected.

Dillinger checked the illuminated dial of his Rolex.

"Give me five minutes, then it's front-door action. Take no prisoners."

"The cavalry's saddled up, Bad One."

"Right," Dillinger grunted. The white-haired man stepped out of the rented '86 Camaro. The transfer getaway wheels, a '74 black Trans-Am with 400 horses under the hood, was parked five blocks north near Interstate 95. If there was trouble with the law, Dillinger hoped the Main Man back at Gator Base Burning Bush in the Everglades could pull some strings. If he couldn't . . . well, Dillinger was willing to take his chances. Over the years, he'd discovered that a man walking with a mission of justice in his heart was usually protected by the gods of fate in some ethereal way that he couldn't quite comprehend. It was as if that man were surrounded by an invincible aura, guided by some cosmic force that was using him to make order out of chaos and right some terrible wrong. Dillinger offered a silent prayer to the universe that somebody was smiling down on his rotten backside, and that his sins were going to be overlooked in place of a greater good. In any lethal confrontation, he knew there was more than just savage skill and raw determination to win involved in deciding the outcome. A man needed General Fortune on his side, too. And it didn't hurt to live by a code of honor.

Stepping toward the bouncers, Dillinger sucked in a deep breath of the hot night air, felt the sweat break out on his forehead, trickle like ice water down the back of his neck. The Blood and Guts specials and a pair of brass knuckles in his jacket pocket would see him through the foray. Hopefully. And yeah, the cavalry was right behind him.

A battle was forthcoming, damn right. If Manny Vitelli thought he could dupe the baddest private investigator since Bogie and butcher an innocent young girl in the process . . . well, by Christ, Dillinger thought, the

Babylon III would end up like ancient Sodom and Gomorrah. In flames. In ruins. In disgrace.

"Evening, boys," Dillinger greeted the bouncers. "I'll get right to the point, so there's no confusion here." As the goons exchanged arrogant glances with each other, Dillinger unzipped his windbreaker, displayed the .45 specials. He kept a safe distance of five feet from the bouncers. "I can draw these .45s in the time it takes either one of you to fart in panic," the white-haired, granite-faced ex-gumshoe hissed through tightly clenched teeth. "They've got hair triggers and a fart in panic might just end up pumping a slug through your faces."

Shock, anger paralyzed the bouncers. Then brutal arrogance fought for control of their expressions.

"What the hell is this?" one of the goons, a giant with shoulder-length curly blond hair, growled.

"I wanna see Manny about an overdue tab, that's what this is about, Goldilocks."

"Hey, wait a minute," the other bouncer rasped. "You're the guy that—"

"That's right, friend. I'm *that* guy you betrayed with your Judas Ben Franklins. Do an about-face. Keep your distance. I'm feeling every bit as mean and ugly as I look."

"You're making a mistake, wiseguy. You see, you go bulling inside, sporting those pistols like you're something out of Tombstone, there's only one way you're going back out. In a plastic bag."

"I hear ya, and I'm not impressed with your tough-guy routine, sport. Now, move it out, Wyatt. Mouth shut. Face front. Any shit, and your guts will be decorating some dancer's belly button."

Inside, Dillinger took in his surroundings with a scathing eye. If it weren't for the seriousness of his "night call," Dillinger might have let his hormones get the best of him. At least two dozen naked women were gyrating to the heavy metal thunder of rock music. Lust-crazed patrons swilled beer and stuffed the garters of the dancers with dollar bills. Strobe lights, suspended from a glass ceiling, flashed. A raining kaleidoscope of color glittered over the long glass stage that bisected the floor, light that seemed to illuminate the women on stage as if they were goddesses that had stepped out of a man's wildest sexual fantasies. Thick shag carpet. One mahogany bar that half-circled the stage. Racks and racks of liquor bottles. Cocktail waitresses with nothing on but a garter and high heels. Christ, he thought, trailing the two goons, women, women, and more women. Young, beautiful women. Blondes, brunettes, redheads. Legs and butt and . . . Zac Dillinger longed for one night he could live it up here. Vitelli had a class place, even if he was nothing more than a worm pimping women, running dope, and selling murder for the mob, Dillinger decided. If he wasn't real careful, Dillinger knew he just might end up dying here, stretched out before some beautiful naked blonde with about a dozen bullet holes gushing blood all over her feet. Then again, he realized he'd just thrown all caution to the wind. And maybe, just maybe, he grimly thought, there were worse ways to go.

The night call, right. The mission. He steeled his mind.

Paula Jessup. Tabs. Vengeance.

Justice. Blood justice.

Death, Bad Zac Dillinger knew, had come to hammer down on the Babylon III.

Chapter 2

Weaving his way through the crowd, Dillinger fixed grim attention on his two reluctant escorts. Walking tall, those two henchmen, Dillinger sensed, seemed confident that they would be able to deal with a lone gun-wielding invader. In time. They were just giving this white-haired wonder, Dillinger thought, a little rope. Elsewhere, Dillinger spotted at least ten other soldiers, standing with arms folded around the bar, talking with waitresses near the stage. Soldiers, because there were bulges beneath the tuxedos of those goons. Dillinger noticed several of those soldiers looking his way. With the front door unattended, it wouldn't take but a few seconds for their suspicion to mount.

The goons led Dillinger beneath a glass archway, and the ex-P.I. glimpsed a reflection of his ugly warhorse mug. For damn sure, he wasn't getting any younger. Lately, he'd been feeling old, and very, very tired. But tired of what? Life? Himself? The Manny Vitellis of the world? He wasn't really sure, and he wasn't sure he wanted to know. At the moment, he was a man with a mission, and that was all that mattered.

They stepped into a darkened area, closed down on a door. Rock music, laughter, and loud talk bombarding his backside, Dillinger unleathered one of his Blood and Guts specials as two more goons guarding the door stiffened, feral aggression darkening their eyes.

8

"I take it Manny's on the other side?" Dillinger said, leveling the .45 Colt on a soldier beside the door.

"Who the fuck are you?" the other goon rasped.

"Never mind, Pete," Goldilocks said. "Just stay cool, huh."

That was all that was said. And Dillinger detected the undertone of cunning in Goldilocks's voice. Dillinger knew he was a problem that would be dealt with in due course.

"Open the door, and file in," Dillinger ordered. "Get cute and I get to mow down one goonsquad. It wouldn't just make my day, either, it would make my year. And it's been one fucking lousy year."

The door was opened. As the henchmen filed through the doorway, Dillinger slipped the fingers of his left hand through the brass knuckles. Entering the room, shutting the door behind him with the heel of a steel-tipped commando boot, the ex-P.I. found Manny Vitelli stretched out on a table. There was a white towel around the mob boss's waist, and two blond vixens, naked except for high heels, were giving Vitelli a thorough body massage. Vitelli and his vixens were all smiles until they saw the white-haired, granite-faced man with the .45 Colt and brass knuckles. Looking over at the white-haired intruder, the blondes' breasts stopped jiggling.

Zac Dillinger became the focus of angry attention. And sudden violence.

Vitelli, a slight man with matted black hair on his shoulders and back, swung his legs off the table. "Hey. . ."

The intended knockout punch was telegraphed, all the way. Combat senses on full alert, Dillinger saw the rage explode in the eyes of the goon to his left-front, saw the tightening of the lips, the stiffening of the shoulders. All the signs of a guy having trouble reacting with deadly cool to a damburst of adrenaline. Dillinger ducked, the backhand hammerfist grazing the top of his head. Teeth bared in a snarl, the ex-P.I. drove the muzzle of his Blood and Guts special into the goon's gut. There was a loud but muffled retort as Dillinger squeezed the trigger, the .45 hollowpoint belching a bloody exit hole the size of a fist out the henchman's back. Pivoting, Dillinger sledgehammered a left uppercut off the jaw of the goon to his right. Jawbone and teeth shattered like thin ice, and that guy crumpled to the floor, down and out for the ten count.

Goldilocks was smattered with blood and tattered strips of cloth as the first Babylon KIA tumbled to the carpet at his feet. Goldilocks looked set to charge the white-haired man, but Dillinger trained the smoking .45 on him in a rock-steady grip. Vitelli obviously didn't pay Goldilocks enough to risk surviving a .45 disembowelment.

"Remember me, Manny?" Realizing he was set on full-scale destruction, in the mood to take the night by vengeance, Dillinger pistoned a sidekick into the breadbasket of Goldilocks. The big blond goon doubled over, and Dillinger whiplashed the barrel of the .45 across the face of the fourth henchman, splitting his nose open in a spray of crimson froth. That goon folded to his knees, hands clutching his mangled nose, tears streaming from his eyes. A real tough guy there, Dillinger thought. Whatever, he now had two fewer problems he'd have to deal with shortly. If nothing else, they'd at least know he wasn't someone to take lightly.

"You son of a bitch!" Vitelli stormed. "What's the meaning of this?"

The floor littered with Dillinger's means to an end, the white-haired man took long strides toward the mob boss. The blondes were rooted to the floor in terror. With a wave of his gun, Dillinger backed the women away from the table.

"That's me, Manny. A rotten son of a bitch, right to the core of my ugly black heart. At the moment, though, I'm a bill collector. And I'm collecting for one Paula Jessup. You remember nineteen-year-old Paula Jessup, don't you, Manny? They found her nude body washed up on the beach in Lauderdale yesterday, Manny. And she didn't die of natural causes. But we both know that, don't we, Manny?" Swiftly, Dillinger moved behind Vitelli. He fisted a handful of the mobster's black hair, wrenched him down on the table, and jammed the .45's muzzle in his mouth, snapping off two of Vitelli's front teeth. Blood spilled down the mobster's chin. Naked fear stared up at Dillinger. For a second, Dillinger wondered if that was how Paula Jessup felt, how she looked to her executioners when she knew the end had come. An idea then formed in Dillinger's mind. The money he was owed no longer meant a thing. Not a damn thing. Dillinger was staring down scum, a whore of life. A user. A taker. A killer at heart who pulled the strings and murdered from the safety of shadows. A coward with money who could make the weak and wanton cater to his whims and desires, garbage who kept a tenuous grip on a glass empire through brutality and treachery.

Vitelli squirmed, and Dillinger rammed the muzzle another inch down the mobster's throat. Vitelli gagged.

"I . . . I don't know what . . . you're talking about," Vitelli sputtered around gunmetal.

Dillinger glanced around the room. Big mahogany desk. Mahogany walls lined with framed pictures of Manny with movie stars and starlets, portraits of mobsters with women on each arm. There were swarthy-looking guys in white suits with pearly-white smiles lighting up their faces and eyes. Colombians, most likely. The jet set. The yachting bunch.

The living dead.

"You killed Paula Jessup, Manny. Had me track her down for you, used me like toilet paper. You can see now that doesn't set right with me, huh. Tell Goldilocks to open the safe I know you've got in here." Dillinger pulled the .45 out of Vitelli's mouth. Wrapping an arm around

Vitelli's throat, Dillinger hauled the mobster off the table, pressed the muzzle to his temple.

"Do it!" Vitelli snapped through his shattered mouth, spitting blood on the plush brown carpet. "Listen to me, you bastard," the mobster rasped. "You think anybody gives a shit what happened to Paula Jessup? She turned out to be nothin' but a cheap whore who didn't have nothin' till she met me. What Manny Vitelli gives, Manny Vitelli takes away, ya understand me?"

"Perfectly."

"Hey, hotshot P.I., you think the cops care about a slut like Paula Jessup? Hell, even if they did give a damn, it won't go any further than today's headline on page four. I own half the fucking pigs in this town, Dillinger! Ya hear me? You ain't shit!"

No, Dillinger couldn't really believe what he was hearing, even though he'd expected nothing less, and nothing more. A full confession, with no remorse, no regret. But Dillinger had already passed a death sentence down on Manny Vitelli. Finally, Dillinger looked at Goldilocks, who hadn't moved a muscle.

"I thought you told your fair-haired boy to do something for me, Manny?"

"What the fuck you waiting for? Get his goddamn money!"

Goldilocks hesitated, as if waiting to see if Vitelli would change his mind. A scowl from Vitelli, then the soldier removed one of the pictures. Moments later, the wall safe was opened.

"You owe me ten grand, Manny," Dillinger reminded the mob boss. "Let's start peeling off those big bills . . . or somebody'll be peeling your brains off the wall."

Vitelli nodded at Goldilocks. The henchman peeled off ten grand, flipped the money down on Manny's desktop. Dillinger moved behind the desk. Viciously, Dillinger thrust Vitelli to his knees. With the back of his knee,

Dillinger pinned Vitelli to the desk. Quickly, the ex-P.I. separated the bills, all of them clean, crisp Grants and Franklins. Dillinger took a brass Zippo from his jacket pocket.

"This is what I think of you and your money, Manny." Dillinger flicked the Zippo, torched half of the bills. As the money burned, he added, "Your money's no good, Manny. Not to me. Not for Paula Jessup. And not to anybody once word of our little encounter of the discomforting kind spreads around town. Then, big man, *you* ain't gonna be worth shit."

"You're a dead man, Dillinger, ya hear me? You won't live through the hour, I'll see to that myself. You're finished. Dead meat."

Dillinger scooped up the other half of the bills and stuffed the money into Vitelli's mouth. "You say something, Manny? That's what I thought." With a crooked smile, Dillinger looked at Goldilocks. "God damn, but I feel good. How 'bout you, sweetheart? You ever think about getting a haircut? You look like one of those punks in a blue boy movie, y'know that? You ever done some head-bobbing, Goldilocks? You look like the type to do some head-bobbing." Hauling Vitelli to his feet by a handful of hair, Dillinger shoved the mob boss across the room. "Okay, Manny, here's the deal. We walk to the front door. Any gunmetal starts flashing, I pump a bullet through your head—you drop towel and die naked right in your own joint."

Dillinger checked his Rolex. Four minutes, forty-five seconds. And counting down. The doomsday numbers were tumbling fast.

A grim realist, Dillinger knew Vitelli's soldiers weren't going to just let him walk out of there without having something to say about it.

Cursing around the wad of bills in his mouth, Vitelli kept the towel clutched around his waist as Dillinger manhandled the mobster toward the door. There, Dillinger opened the door, the muzzle of his .45 dug into the nape of Vitelli's neck. Head twisted sideways, Dillinger kept an eye on Goldilocks, who was simmering with rage and humiliation.

Suddenly, the soldier with the broken jaw stirred to life. Eyes clearing then burning with anger, he clawed for gunmetal. A split second later, the Colt Python .357 Magnum tracked to draw a bead on Dillinger's backside.

One of the blondes screamed, alerting Dillinger to the threat of being backshot.

The .45 automatic streaking to draw target acquisition in the blink of an eye, Zac Dillinger stroked the hair trigger of the Blood and Guts special. The pearl-handled Colt bucked in his fist, cannoned a .45 hollowpoint slug that turned the gunman's face into crimson mush.

Doomsday now threatened to hammer Zac Dillinger into the ground.

All eyes in the Babylon III were turned toward Dillinger and his hostage. The relentless barrage of rock and roll music was the only sound in the strip bar.

Adrenaline burning through his veins, Dillinger shoved Vitelli beneath the archway. Something glinted in the glass overhead Dillinger. A light.

Gunmetal.

And Dillinger reacted to the danger with the speed of a lightning bolt.

Pivoting, Dillinger saw the soldier crouched in a doorway to his left. The Ingram M10 stuttered, spitting flame and lead. But Dillinger had cleared the tracking line of fire.

Manny Vitelli became an unwitting shield as the line of .45 ACP slugs marched up his right leg. The mobster screamed, thrashed in Dillinger's arms, and the towel fell to the floor. Twice, Dillinger caressed the hair trigger of the Blood and Guts special. One .45 round opened a window to the subgunner's brains. The second slug puked off a tuft of his skull. Slicked in his own juices, the subgunner whirled, crashed into the wall.

And blood trailed Vitelli in a gory spray, the mobster howling, grabbing at his leg, unmindful of his stark nakedness. Bills loosened in Vitelli's mouth, fluttered to the floor.

Then all hell really broke loose, and Dillinger found himself wedged in a lethal crossfire hurricane of lead.

Patrons nose-dived to the floor. Waitresses, screaming in terror, were bowled down by men seeking cover. Glasses and bottles whirled through the air, shattering all over the floor.

His timing perfect, Johnny Simms barged through the doors, twin Little Lightnings drawn and looking for enemy blood.

The goons in front of the bar hit instant combat crouches behind the railing and tables. Big handguns were tracking Dillinger, and slugs began booming from those cannons.

"Nooooo! You dumbfucks, noooooo!" Vitelli bellowed.

Either they felt the situation was beyond hope, their pride was tarnished, or they didn't give a damn one way or another if Manny Vitelli lived or died, Dillinger wasn't certain. In the underworld, a fresh face was always welcome in the mob as the lower ranks of competition slugged it out to be head cock of the pecking order. Perhaps Manny, Dillinger thought, had outlived his usefulness, and one of the soldiers in that strip joint was looking to fill his shoes. Whatever, Dillinger flung Vitelli behind a pillar, more for his own protection than out of any concern for the mobster's safety. Shards of glass exploded beside Dillinger's face as heavy-caliber bullets rained down on his position.

Johnny Simms braced himself against the wall just inside the doorway. The black merc shaved the odds a fraction as he mowed down two gunmen behind the railing, doubled-fisted Little Lightnings burping out a hot stream of 9mm lead. Blood and brains burst from skulls, and faces twisted in agony. Death masks with sightless staring eyes were trampled into pulp by patrons fleeing for cover behind the bar.

A goon slid out from behind a pillar, his .44 Magnum thundering lead that cleaved off wood beside the black merc's face. Flinching, Simms belly flopped in the doorway. Jutting the mini-Uzis around the corner, Simms stitched the gunman from crotch to throat with double-fisted lead sizzlers. Tracking on, Simms pinned another Mafia soldier to the front of the bar with double 3-round bursts, the goon's tux chopped up into a bloody rag by sizzling 9mm lead hornets.

Unleathering his second .45 automatic, Dillinger drew target acquisition on a soldier racing down behind the bar above the stage.

Another goon reeled to the stage as Simms opened his chest with a crimson figure eight. The guy slid in his own juices as blood showered over the glass stage. Dancers scattered pell-mell away from the fresh corpse, shrieking at the top of their lungs, unmindful of the dollar bills that flew from their garters in their haste to escape the brutal firefight.

Both .45s flaming and bucking in his hands, Dillinger caught another soldier in the ear with two bullets. At the moment, Dillinger had only one thing in mind. *Get the hell out of here*. Bad Zac had made his point, and he figured Paula Jessup had been avenged.

Almost.

Manny Vitelli was looking up at the white-haired man with hate-filled eyes. He cursed Dillinger. It was the last thing Manny Vitelli ever did.

"For Paula, Manny. The tab's paid up," Zac Dillinger said, and he pumped one slug into Vitelli's face. "And

Manny," he snarled down at the twitching corpse, "I cared."

At a glance, Dillinger spotted the plate-glass window on the second tier just beyond the pillar. Simms was already ramming home fresh 32-round clips into his Little Lightnings. Using the split-second lull to muster courage, the goons at the bar began raking Simms's position with Magnum lead.

A revolver, though, Dillinger watched to his delight, is no match for a weapon that can pound out 1,200 rounds per minute. *Make that 2,400 rounds per minute,* Dillinger thought, streaking away from the pillar as Simms opened up with another Little Lightning fusillade on the gunmen at the bar. And kicked two fresh corpses back into the racks of liquor.

The din of autofire, shattering glass, and high-pitched female screams in his ears, Dillinger bounded over a table, vaulted the railing, surprised at his own Olympic-like agility. Fear of death, though, could turn a beer-swilling two-hundred-pound slug into Jesse Owens in the blink of an eye, Dillinger grimly realized as he heard a slug whine off the railing behind him, then felt the lead hornet sting his earlobe. Suddenly, the plate-glass window in front of Dillinger spiderwebbed under the onslaught of heavy-caliber lead. Leaving his feet, shielding his face with his forearms, Dillinger missiled through the window. A tidal wave of glass shards typhooned over Dillinger as he hit the sidewalk on his side. Breaking out of his roll, Dillinger bolted to his feet.

Simms was already running across the parking lot.

Dillinger dived through the open passenger window of the Camaro. Simms opened the driver's-side door, slamming it with a vengeance, it seemed, as he hopped in behind the wheel. As Simms revved the engine to life, Dillinger triggered another .45 slug as a soldier barged through the doors, the goon's .357 Magnum up and tracking.

The guy dropped in his tracks, poleaxed as the .45 slug tunneled open his guts.

Simms's face was sheened with sweat. "Don't ever, *ever, ever* ask me out for a few beers again, goddamn you, you understand me! This is the kinda shit I have nightmares about. The world's got enough trouble without us goin' and lookin' for it."

Simms peeled the Camaro out of the parking lot on a screech of rubber.

Dillinger holstered his Blood and Guts specials. He checked the sideview mirror. No sign of the law. Yet. No sirens. Yet. It was then that he tasted the blood in his mouth. A deep gash had been opened in the top of his head from his dive through the glass.

"Relax, Johnny Boy," Bad Zac Dillinger said gruffly. "I didn't promise you the Babylon III was going to be any fucking rose garden. C'mon, the night's young. Where's your spunk, huh? Let's go grab a beer."

Simms muttered a curse, shook his head.

The palm fronds rustled in the hot breeze. Two dark shadows detached themselves from the corner of the Babylon III.

"Interesting," commented the big man with the crew cut and bullet-shaped head, his gaze narrowing over cold gray eyes as he watched the Camaro vanish into the gloom down the sidestreet.

"I would say enlightening," added the slightly built man with a beaked nose and closely cropped black hair. "Special Operations will be most pleased with our trackdown, friend Torquemada."

"After the Tunisian affair, friend Sprenger, there's only one way to go."

Right, the CIA operative code-named Sprenger thought. One way to go. Down. Into the abyss.

"Radio ahead to the others, friend Torquemada,"

Sprenger said. "Wherever they go when they change to that Trans-Am . . . we will follow. Whoever loses them . . . they will answer to me."

In the aftermath of the firefight, men were scrambling out the front doors, staggering like drunks in fear of what they'd just witnessed.

"They're good," Torquemada said as sirens wailed in the distance.

"They're ambitious men albeit dangerous. But what did friend Napoleon say about ambition?"

"Ambition is bad for the character. I quote, 'Crimes are no more to it than games. Ambition is never content, even on the summit of greatness.'"

"And they saw their summit in Tunisia."

"Not yet," Torquemada said. "They have one more summit of greatness to climb. A half a world away. In a land that time and the rest of the world have forgotten."

"Indeed." Sprenger's jaw tightened, a look of deadly intent steeling his gray eyes. "One final climb to greatness. Then . . ."

"A plunge to death."

"Their own ambition, friend Torquemada, will be their Waterloo. We will see to it."

The big man was silent. Sirens klaxoned closer to the hell zone.

The palm fronds trembled behind Sprenger and Torquemada.

Death, Sprenger thought, will stalk them all once again after tonight. And the commandos he had tracked down since the Tunisian massacre of the Sword of Islam, he knew, would feel Death's poisonous sting. Of that much, Sprenger was certain.

Chapter 3

Trouble was nothing new to Vic Gabriel. Neither was the former CIA assassin a virgin to danger or bad news. Since his days with the Special Forces in Vietnam, he had carried a bellyful of painful memories as the result of years from living on the knife's edge of trouble, danger, and worse than bad news. In a way, he realized that pain either made a man or broke him down into self-pitying stagnation. A warrior, he believed, used pain to steel his heart, make him aware of his abilities and limitations, cement a code of honor and form a philosophy that would carry him through the dark times. For the warrior, pain, then, was needed. How pain was dealt with was one way to separate a warrior from the rest of the human pack.

And Vic Gabriel didn't mind trouble either. Trouble was adversity to be overcome. What Vic Gabriel didn't need was for any of the three commandos of Eagle Force to go in search of trouble. Zac Dillinger, to Gabriel's anger and disbelief, had done just that with his stunt in Miami last night.

To take his mind off Dillinger, Gabriel concentrated on rigging the last of the spring snares along the edge of the mangrove forest. After the slaughter of the Sword of Islam in Tunisia, Gabriel figured it was wise to base Eagle Force at the southern end of the Florida Everglades. Taking an extended furlough to recover from their wounds inflicted by the enemy during battle, Eagle Force had then gone to work ringing the perimeter of the base with electronic surveillance equipment. As added precautions, the team had set up trip wires, cameras, and—provided an intruder broke through the outer ring of defense—exactly one hundred animal traps to snare bad company. Expensive equipment, and elaborate defensive measures, right. But thanks to their first and now late principal, Bradley Milton III, Eagle Force had netted in excess of two hundred thousand dollars cash, so there was plenty of money to burn on the necessities of survival. Indeed, secrecy about the base and ironclad insurance against intruders was a must. A *must*, Gabriel knew, because of his past involvement with the CIA.

Behind him, Gabriel heard the blister of autofire. Turning his head sideways, Gabriel watched the two men in combat fatigues as they worked out on the war course.

Johnny Simms, the bullet- and soul-scarred ex-merc with clandestine combat experience in Central America, hit the soft turf behind a line of sandbags, rolled, and sprang up into a combat crouch. Triggering his AR-18 assault rifle on the run, Simms pumped concentrated 3-round bursts of .223 Remington lead into man-sized targets a dozen yards downrange. Simms stitched perfect figure eights in the chests of four dummies. Even though his camos were slicked with mud, Simms's AR-18 was spotless. Just one sign of the real pro, Gabriel knew. Dirty weapons got jammed. Jammed weapons got a man killed. While free-lancing his martial skills for the CIA in Central America, Gabriel had fought alongside Simms against communist guerrillas. Simms was good, Gabriel knew, and the black ex-merc had a fifth-degree blackbelt to add to his deadly talents with an assault rifle or knife.

Intently eyeing the workout, Gabriel saw Henry van Boolewarke, the big, crew cut ex-Recces commando, loose an arrow from his all-metal Barnett Panzer crossbow. The broadhead arrowpoint streaked on-target, *thunking* a millisecond later in the chest of another dummy. No sooner had he scored that potentially lethal hit, Henry van Boolewarke was already loading the crossbow. Sometimes Gabriel would swear he detected a glimmer of affection in Boolewarke's eyes whenever he looked at the crossbow. For the Barnett Panzer crossbow was inscribed with the name of Boolewarke's father, and the former South African commando didn't go anywhere, it seemed, without the cherished killpiece slung around his shoulder. And Gabriel knew the Afrikaner could impale a living, moving target from dozens of yards away with the Barnett Panzer. Had seen it during the massacre of the Sword of Islam.

Even outside the fields of slaughter, Vic Gabriel was proud of his commandos, trusted and respected them. They weren't fighting for money or glory. They weren't kill-crazy psychos searching for thrills and longing to taste blood. No. It went far and above personal gain, thrillseeking, and even vengeance in the name of justice. In Vic Gabriel's mind, the world was in trouble, assaulted daily by the savage hordes of international terrorists and criminals. Someone had to make a stand before the savages devoured all innocent flesh. Someone had to take the fire to the barbarian throngs and drive that fire down their throats. Someone with lethal martial skill, guts, and raw determination, right. Someone who could slay the enemy without blinking an eye, but who could still feel compassion for his fellow men who wanted to live a good and decent life free from terror and hate. Some men are called to act but never hear the calling, Vic Gabriel believed. He'd been called, due in large part to the ghosts of terrible memories, born in the hellstorm of a nightmarish past. Yeah, he'd heard the calling, and he was going in for the kill, damn right. Governments of the free world appeared impotent in the war against terrorism. Call it conscience trouble. Call it politics. Call it greed, graft, and corruption. Whatever, none of the four commandos of Eagle

Force were handcuffed by any law other than an eye for an eye. Or rather, where the terrorists were concerned—*two eyes for an eye*. All right, so maybe just a touch of vengeance was involved. Vic Gabriel would be the first one to admit that a part of him felt good when the terrorists started swallowing their own brand of twisted poison. And if he wasn't fighting to make the world just a little safer, he would sure as hell wish that there was somebody else out there to do the grim work in his place. The only way to deal with terrorists, he knew, was to erase them from the face of the earth. Forever. *The only good terrorist is a dead terrorist*.

If any of the other Eagle Force commandos felt differently, then they were the best damn actors and con men he'd ever seen, Gabriel thought. Con men, though, they weren't. They were real. And they had heart.

Johnny Simms had left behind a life of hustling pool and fighting in backstreet alleys for a buck to become a member of the team. Okay, Gabriel admitted to himself, so just what kind of life had that been anyway? Perhaps Simms, he realized, had merely left one thrill behind for another. Any way it was sliced, the black ex-merc was tried and true. With three tours of the Nam under his belt, Simms had been destined, Gabriel believed, to end up right there in the Florida Everglades. Soldiering was all he knew. Killing was all he was going to see until he checked out. And Johnny Simms believed in the justice of their war against terrorism. It was never so much in what a man said, Gabriel knew, but in what he *did*.

Henry van Boolewarke, Gabriel thought, was an Eagle Force commando by way of tragedy. Of Boer descent, the Dutchman had felt he'd been left with no choice after the massacre in the Transvaal, a grim, bloody battle that had changed his life forever. And perhaps fate had thrown Boolewarke into the eye of a firestorm because of his lineage and the color of his skin. For a brief moment,

Gabriel recalled the gruesome aftermath he'd seen that day in the Transvaal. The trackdown of the Afrikaner had led Gabriel straight into the bowels of hell on earth. A sight of horror he would not soon forget. The Dutchman's ranch, reduced to cinders after a furious two-day battle with guerrillas of the African National Congress. Fire-shriveled or bullet-riddled corpses strewn across the hell zone, rotting under a setting sun while the vultures gathered to feast on dead flesh. With his ranch burned to the ground, with his workers all dead and with his dream in life shattered, Boolewarke had, with some reservations, accepted Gabriel's contract for slaughter against the Arab terrorist group the Sword of Islam, in Tunisia. Part of Boolewarke accepted the deal because the Dutchman claimed he owed Gabriel. It was no false claim. Years ago, Gabriel almost single-handedly wiped out three squads of Russian-Cuban killers that had ambushed Boolewarke and other Recce commandos in Angola. Back then, Gabriel had worked for the Company as an assassin. He'd been in Angola to terminate a notorious SPETSNAZ major general who was using the country as a springboard for terrorist attacks against South Africa. But Gabriel knew Boolewarke was motivated by more than just despair when he'd joined the team. A captain doesn't go down with his ship unless he gives a damn about the crew. Boolewarke had fought down to the last man during those two days of bitter fighting in the Transvaal, in a valiant effort to save not just his ranch and his dream, but to defend the lives of the people who had lived with him and worked the ranch. If Gabriel knew Boolewarke didn't give a damn about people, didn't believe he could do something to right some serious wrongs in the world, he would never have asked the Dutchman to join Eagle Force.

Gabriel covered over the spring snare with brush, stood. There was a .45 Colt ACP in Gabriel's hip holster. The heavy firepower was housed in the command post at the edge of the pier. Assault rifles. Machine guns. Automatic shotguns. Grenade and rocket launchers. Thousands of rounds of ammunition. All the firepower they would need to head out for the next killing field. Wherever and whatever that call might be.

"That should do it," Gabriel said, then shook free a Marlboro from a rumpled pack. Flicking a gold-plated Zippo, Gabriel fired up the smoke. Engraved on the Zippo was a death's-head. An inscription beneath the death's-head read, *7th SFG—no compromise.*

Covering branches over the noose of another spring snare, Zac Dillinger looked up at Gabriel. For a moment, the two men stared at each other. There was a stretched second of heavy silence. Since learning from Dillinger about the firefight at the Babylon III, then reading about it the next morning in the *Miami Herald*, Gabriel had chewed the ex-P.I. out more than once. The only evidence that Dillinger had even been involved in the Babylon III battle was the line of stitches Boolewarke had sewn across the top of his forehead. Even now, Dillinger was still spitting out glass chips from his dive through the window of the Babylon III. Okay, Gabriel had to give the guy credit for guts, even though he sat on his brains once in a while.

"You look a little embarrassed to me, Zac. If you're not, maybe you oughta be. Think?"

Dillinger stood, a bone in his knee cracking, as he rested a hand over the pearl-handled butt of one of his .45 specials. "C'mon, VG, you're not still sore at me about last night, are ya?" A sheepish grin creased his lips. "Hell, pal, how can you stay pissed off at a lovable old warhorse like me anyway? Me and you went through the conveyor belt of death down there in the bush and came back to tell about it. We understand that life's shit-cheap and that the Paula Jessups of the world don't count in the eyes of most people. I would've at least expected you to try and understand that I felt a debt was owed to someone who didn't deserve to end up like that kid."

"Believe me, Zac, I understand a lot better than you think. You're just not listening to what I've already said. Maybe you heard, but you're too caught up seeing your own side of it. And you're starting to piss me off."

"What about honor, huh?"

"I've heard of it," Gabriel said, his voice edged with sarcasm.

"What about pride?"

"It's in the dictionary between prickly pear and prie-dieu."

"What's a prie-dieu?"

"I think it's something like a prima donna who runs off half-cocked shooting up titty bars, all in the name of honor and pride."

Dillinger's eyes hardened with anger. "If I didn't know you the way I do, Gabriel, I'd . . . I'd . . . fuck it."

"Yeah, fuck it."

Gabriel drew deep on his smoke to try to calm the anger threatening to knot up his guts. Dillinger was perhaps the only one of them who would openly invite trouble. Kicking ass was just in Dillinger's blood, but Gabriel wasn't about to cut the ex-P.I. any slack because of a wild hair. Sure, maybe the very nature of what they all did was nothing more than a one-way ticket for a front-row seat with Death. If trouble was what Dillinger wanted, Gabriel knew he could send the guy to a hundred different hot spots around the globe to face more . . . ah, the hell with it, Gabriel decided. The former private investigator still didn't seem to understand the risk he'd run by going after Manny Vitelli in his personal vendetta. Gabriel figured he might as well go beat his brains out with a hammer.

Softly, Gabriel shook his head. "You don't get it, do you, Zac? You just don't seem to understand."

"Look, Vic, I already explained—more than once, I

might add, for Christ sake. I owed that son of a bitch Vitelli, in the worst way. And despite how you feel about it, I'm glad I did it. You know how many guys like Vitelli just walk all over people's lives every day and there's nobody there to stand up to these pricks, huh? Jesus Christ, Vic, I thought that's what this was all about anyway. Fighting for the little people who can't fight back. If I can't care a little, if I can't give back a little, then I'm really not worth spit."

"Yeah, Zac, I've heard your plea. More than once—I might add. But let me ask you—did you do it for Paula Jessup, or yourself?"

Dillinger looked resentful for a moment, then his brow furrowed and he appeared to choose his words carefully. "To tell you the truth, Vic, at first, I guess I was doing it for me. That was until I got in the joint and came face-to-face with the scumbag. The whole time I was going through the motions of moving in on the creep . . . hell, I got to thinking of what it must've been like for that kid. Scared. Screwed up. A runaway, it turns out. Looking for a little piece of the good life but not really understanding the price tag that comes with the search and the hunger for that life until it's too late. I dunno, Vic. Part of me did it for me, all right . . . the other part did it for her. But hell, VG, you tell me, and you know that usually there's always more than one reason why a man does something. Nobody's that goddamned noble."

Gabriel began walking across the grass field, heading toward the two wooden buildings that sat at the east end of the pier. One of the buildings was their command post, the other building the barracks for sleeping. An airboat was tied to the pier, the team's only way out of the Everglades. Beyond the pier stretched the tough saw grass of the Everglades. Some thirty kilometers northeast was a remote heliport. There, an ex-Nam gunship pilot by the name of Tommy Wilson owned a Bell 222. Wilson had already received a hefty advance to fly any of the members of Eagle Force to the coast whenever they needed something or felt the urge for some human contact. Dillinger had already taken full advantage of that arrangement, and Gabriel was regretting the money he'd handed over to Wilson for services paid in advance. His heart gripped by annoyance and worry, there was a stink in the hot air, a smell of decay that Gabriel suddenly noticed, and he let his senses as well as his soul become assaulted by the environment. In some respects, Gabriel thought, the swamp is like the jungle. The life cycle. The hunter and the hunted. The dead and the dying. The eternal struggle between life forces for survival. Was man, Gabriel wondered, that much unlike the animal life of the swamp and the jungle? It wasn't really all that true that just the strong survived. No, the weak survived, too; they merely lived like honing stones for the appetites of the strong, being fattened to be preyed upon when the time was right.

As Gabriel headed across the field, Dillinger right beside him, he listened to the roar of Simms's AR-18, felt the sun beating down on his neck and face as the bloodred orb sank closer to the treeline of the cypress and mangrove forest.

"My only concern, Zac," Gabriel said, blowing smoke out his nose, his eyes hard, his boots squishing through the marshy turf, "is you bringing the mob down on our asses before we ever get the chance to get this thing off the ground. One mission under the belt doesn't mean any of us are heroes. I don't believe in resting on my last success."

"Hey, no sweat, VG," Dillinger assured. "No mob boys will come stalking around."

"So you say."

"So I mean, dammit," Dillinger growled. "Listen, we

got away clean. Our boy, Tommy, over at the heliport, lifted me and Johnny here, safe and sound."

"That doesn't mean you, *we* can't be found. And what about our boy, Tommy, anyway? Somebody could get to him. For a few dollars more, he might start squawking loud enough to be heard up and down the Atlantic seaboard. 'Oh, yeah, I know those boys. Jeez, you guys pay good, better than that tight-fisted SOB, Gabriel. Yeah, I heard about the Babylon III. Yeah, I think I love ya. Damn, that wad of cash looks good.'"

Wood groaned as Gabriel and Dillinger stepped up onto the pier. Gabriel spotted a scaly snout edging through the water's surface beyond the command post. Two black eyes stared up at Gabriel for a second, then the gator slid through the water, angling away from the pier. Gabriel flicked his butt into the water.

"I'm tellin' ya, Vic, you've got nothing to worry about. If we were going to be found out because of last night, it would've happened before now."

Gabriel grunted. Right. Then he heard it. A familiar hum that grew into a buzz within seconds. Both men froze on the pier. They stared at the wavering saw grass, then spotted the giant blades in the distance as the trio of airboats knifed through the water. Gabriel and Dillinger exchanged worried glances.

"Who the hell are these guys?"

"You tell me," Gabriel rasped. "Maybe our boy, Tommy, needed some extra cash. Maybe he wanted to take a trip to the Bahamas and leave us stranded in the Everglades. Shit!"

"How the hell...what in the..."

Gabriel's anxiety turned to fear a second later. He found himself looking at nine hardmen in the airboats. Worse still, there was a .50-caliber machine gun mounted on the bow of each airboat. Those maneaters were belted, and a hardman stood ready by each of the .50-calibers.

"Trouble, that's all I know. Break out the M-16s, Zac," Gabriel ordered. "The ones with the M203s. Just in case we've got to blow our visitors out of the water."

Without hesitation, Dillinger moved into the command post. Turning, Gabriel saw Simms and Boolewarke running from the war course. Judging from the expressions on their faces, Gabriel knew their grim curiosity was aroused.

Trouble had followed Dillinger to the Everglades, all right.

And Vic Gabriel found himself in one ugly mood.

A killing mood.

Zac Dillinger burst through the doorway of the command post with four M-16 assault rifles with attached M203 grenade launchers. The ex-P.I. tossed Gabriel an M-16.

Chapter 4

They didn't blow their visitors out of the water with a barrage of 40mm grenades. But then Vic Gabriel heard, "CIA. Special Operations Division. We need to talk to you. It's urgent." And Gabriel felt his trigger finger twitching.

"I'm not interested," Gabriel growled. "Turn around and forget this place exists or I'll fill you full of holes and feed your rotten asses to the gators."

Even as those words left his mouth, Gabriel knew that was impossible. They couldn't just leave, but issuing a threat of death never hurt to let his enemies know where they stood with him. Instead of leaving, they could, though, just disappear. And anybody involved with the CIA was Vic Gabriel's enemy.

Their hands raised above their heads, the nine Company operatives stood in the airboats, the big blades slowly spinning to a stop now that the engines had been cut. Gabriel and his Eagle Force commandos kept their M-16s trained on the operatives. All of the Company men wore white windbreakers, black slacks, and dark sunglasses. Their expressions stayed cold, and they stood, motionless, like statues.

"Say, wait a minute," Henry van Boolewarke said, his voice thick with his native tongue, as the Dutchman peered at Torquemada and Sprenger. "Those are the two clowns who were eyeballing us in Tunis, Vic. What the bloody hell is going on here?"

Gabriel wondered that, too. Alarm bells klaxoned in his head. He intended to hear the Company goons out after all. But only for information he could get out of them. Then, he just might find out how hungry an Everglades gator was.

"Yes, we know all about your massacre of the Sword of Islam in Tunisia, Gabriel," Sprenger said, his tone confident, as if he knew he held all the right cards. "We know about the late Bradley Milton III, too, mainly because we steered him in your direction. We know all of your names, we know just who and what you are. We know your pasts, everything about you from the day of your birth to the present. And if you cooperate, the four of you just might have futures and live to be semiwise old men. But only if you deal with us. I repeat, it's urgent that we talk to you. Extremely urgent."

"Talk about what?" Gabriel rasped.

"Hiring you and your men for a very sensitive operation," Torquemada answered. "A recovery operation. One that could well turn into a search-and-destroy mission."

It was all Gabriel could do to keep from ventilating those operatives with a burst from his M-16. More than once, he'd felt the sting of CIA treachery. More than once the CIA had betrayed him and cost him great suffering. *A deal, huh*, he thought. *Talk about signing a pact with the devil*.

"What if I'm not interested?"

"Then, friend Gabriel," Torquemada said, his expression solemn, "you may have just helped to start World War III."

"I don't like it, Vic," Zac Dillinger said gruffly. "We've all had trouble with the CIA before. Now these goons roll in out of nowhere, not even a hair out of place, looking like they're set to audition for a blue boy movie, with some song and dance about World War III. It stinks like this frigging swamp."

A cold smile stretched Torquemada's lips. "You have only yourself to thank for us rolling in out of nowhere, friend Zachary."

"Yes," Sprenger added. "Quite a performance last night at the Babylon III. Next time you should check beneath the fender of your Trans-Am for homing devices if you wish to escape the scene of a crime. And murder, I believe, friend Zachary, is a crime in this state. Perhaps we should go to the authorities with what we witnessed last night?"

Gabriel showed Dillinger an ugly scowl.

"Okay, okay," Dillinger said, catching Gabriel's expression. "I'll never go into town for a couple of beers again, I swear."

"Should you not hear us out, friend Gabriel," Torquemada went on, "we will turn around and leave, yes. And Zachary Dillinger and John Simms will become famous men for their performance last night."

Blackmail time, Gabriel thought. He should've figured the Company would resort to some dirty trick if they wanted something out of him.

"All right, step out, one at a time," Gabriel ordered. Then he told his commandos, "Strip 'em down; bring the two clowns from Carthage inside."

Quickly, the Company ops filed off the airboats, stepped onto the pier. Boolewarke, Simms, and Dillinger frisked the ops.

"Nice stuff," Dillinger said, pulling out a stainless steel .44 AutoMag from a hip holster, then sliding a short, compact Ingram M10 submachine gun out of the special low-riding shoulder holster of another operative. With a casual flip, Dillinger pitched the weapons into the water. As the operatives cursed and grumbled, Boolewarke and Simms threw the rest of the confiscated weapons into the water, too. Walther .380 ACP double-action pieces. Mini-Uzis. Three Grizzly Winchester .45 Magnums.

Dillinger whistled. "They sure came ready to talk, didn't they?"

"Move it out, soldier boys," Simms said, nudging an operative in the back with the muzzle of his M-16. "The captain's all ears. And you'd better pray he likes what he hears."

Inside the command post, Gabriel fired up another Marlboro with a flick of his Zippo. Spartanly furnished, there was only a large wooden table, a sofa, a bookcase filled with history and military books, a refrigerator, and a rack of liquor in the command HQ. Firepower and ammo were stored in three large metal bins with locks. When the command HQ was unattended, an alarm system was switched on to alert Eagle Force to the presence of any invader there. If they were to be gone from the base for any length of time, high-powered explosives would blow any intruder, along with the shack, halfway across the Everglades.

With mounting concern, Gabriel waited as Dillinger and Boolewarke led the two operatives chosen for the parley through the door. Outside, Johnny Simms kept his M-16 trained on the rest of the operatives.

Gabriel blew smoke in the direction of the ops, both of whom left their sunglasses on. Whatever the Company wanted to get them involved in, well, he knew it wouldn't be good. Straight-shooting was not a Company virtue. It could damn well be, he thought, that Eagle Force would get its wings clipped before they ever got a chance to fly again.

"You had to bring along a small army to ask us to do a job?"

"Necessary precautions, in light of the Tunisian affair. I think you understand."

"More than you know," Gabriel said, tight-lipped.

"Allow me to introduce myself. I am Agent Torquemada and this is Agent Sprenger."

Sprenger nodded at Gabriel. Dillinger chuckled, then the ex-P.I. fired up a fat stogie with his brass Zippo and exhaled a thick cloud of smoke that hung in the room like a London fog.

"Appropriate cover names," Boolewarke said, his voice steely. "Did you pick the names of two of history's most notorious torturers out of a hat, or what?"

"It's no coincidence, friend Boolewarke, ex-Recce commando," Sprenger said.

"I bet," Dillinger dryly remarked, chomping on his cigar.

"And you can cut with the bloody *friend* nonsense, chum," Boolewarke growled.

Gabriel got the ball rolling. "All right, what's this about hiring us out?" He checked his Rolex. "You've got two minutes before I kick you back in your boats."

Torquemada reached inside his jacket. "May I?"

"May you what?" Gabriel asked.

Torquemada pulled out a large piece of paper. He unfolded the paper on the table.

"This is a map of Nepal, with the Himalayas sketched in and the recovery area marked in red," Torquemada said. "A very serious crisis has developed in Nepal. One which could ignite a confrontation between the superpowers unless it is taken care of immediately."

"Nepal? The Himalayas?" Dillinger echoed.

"Yeah," Gabriel mused. " 'House of Snow,' or 'Snowy Range.' That's what Himalaya means in Sanskrit."

"I'm getting cold just thinking about it," Dillinger said.

"Is the CIA hunting the abominable snowman?" Boolewarke added with sarcasm.

"Let me guess," Gabriel said. "You need expendables for this recovery excursion halfway around the world."

Torquemada shrugged. "Not an inappropriate choice of words, no."

"Get to the point, goddammit," Gabriel snarled. "If you know about me, then you know I hate the fucking CIA."

"But you have worked for the Company in the past. On a number of occasions," Sprenger pointed out.

"Right," Gabriel growled. "And you know my father was murdered in a bungled hostage rescue mission in Paris as the result of CIA treachery."

"We know all about Colonel Charles Gabriel and his fate at the hands of the errant, and I might add, turncoat operative, Michael Saunders," Sprenger said. "United States Army Special Forces, the colonel played a key role in the conception of the SF in 1952. Your mother, Patricia, a nurse in a MASH unit during the Korean conflict, killed when her base was shelled. Your brother, Jim, draft dodger during the Vietnam war, died from a cocaine overdose. Should I go on?"

Gabriel felt his teeth set on edge. No, the bastard didn't have to go on. It was all coming back now, the painful, gut-wrenching memories. So many lives ago, it seemed, he had lost his father because a CIA operative had gone over the Iron Curtain during the failed Paris rescue mission. Michael Saunders. Hotshot CIA specialist who sold his soul to the highest bidder—Ivan. Gabriel had attempted to track down his father's murderer for years after the disastrous French affair. In vain. All in goddamn vain.

"Your father," Sprenger went on, "was quite a man. It seems he trained you and your brother, Jim, in the Colorado Rockies to be soldiers following the Korean conflict."

"Not just soldiers, *friend*," Gabriel said, his back turned to the ops. "Warriors. There's a big difference in my mind. Now, you can skip the history of my family. You know it, but I know all of it."

Torquemada cleared his throat. "Very well. Let me

continue. Here," he said, and jabbed his finger on the map. "Mount Makalu. At twenty-seven thousand eight hundred and twenty-four feet, Makalu I is the fifth-highest mountain in the world."

"What about it?" Gabriel said gruffly.

"We want you and your men to climb it," Sprenger said, point-blank.

A leaden hush fell over the room. Gabriel, Boolewarke, and Dillinger stared at the ops as if they were crazy.

Gabriel drew on his smoke, chuckled. "Just like that, huh? Just like that Frenchman, what's his name?"

"Friend Jean Franco," Sprenger said. "The first man to reach the summit of Makalu, he did it in 1955."

"Let me explain," Torquemada said.

"Yeah, why don't you," Dillinger said, puffing nervously on his stogie.

"Exactly four days ago, two Company reconnaissance airplanes were on a mission inside Russia, originally flying near the Afghanistan border before they veered off to complete their reconnaissance of the China-Russia border. They were flying new rocket-armed SR-71s. The SR-71, as you may know, is the successor to the U-2, can fly at an altitude of more than eighty-five thousand feet, and is capable of Mach 3 speed for ninety minutes."

"Right, right," Gabriel cut in. "You're breaking Gary Powers's heart with your recitation. I know something about the SR-71. But when did you start arming recon birds with warheads?"

"Since it was feared the Soviets had broken the arms reduction treaties about two months ago," Torquemada replied.

"No news there," Boolewarke said. "Anybody with a half a brain should've known Ivan was just blowing smoke with all that talk about dismantling their nuclear payload pointed at Western Europe and Uncle Sugar. Ivan's just a goddamn liar, a treacherous one at that."

"Maybe dismantling the missiles aimed at Europe, perhaps," Sprenger said. "That doesn't mean the Russians can't move them elsewhere."

"Which is exactly what the SR-71s discovered on their mission," Torquemada said. "A massive shipment to, and a buildup of nuclear missile bases along, the Afghanistan and China border. Worse, an earlier mission delivered photographs of what could be Soviet killer-satellite bases."

"C'mon," Dillinger scoffed. "Now you're gonna stand there and talk to us about Star Wars?"

Sprenger shrugged. "Believe what you will. The fact of the matter is, we've known the Soviets have been working on their own SDI for almost twenty years. The reason, we believe, that the Soviets insist we curtail research into our own, uh, Star Wars program, is because they may be on the verge of a breakthrough. Anyway—"

"Anyway," Torquemada went on, "there was a malfunction in one of the SR-71s. Three of its four Sidewinder missiles were launched, scoring direct hits on one of the Soviet bases. A defect in the new design of the SR-71, it's believed. The SR-71 perhaps just couldn't handle the added weight of the missiles and sustain such a high altitude."

"More like an oversight," Gabriel said. "The damn birds couldn't haul the added weight so they just blew their payloads to unburden themselves instead."

"Unfortunately, it would appear it's something like that," Torquemada said. "Whatever, the last radio transmission from Captain Thomas Blackwell indicated that extensive damage was done to one of the Soviet bases along the Chinese border. Soviet MiGs then proceeded to chase our people clear across the northwestern corner of China, through Tibet."

"And a dogfight at forty-five thousand feet over the Himalayas took place," Gabriel threw in. "What about the pilots?"

"We don't know for certain," Sprenger answered. "There's a possibility that Captain Blackwell ejected from his plane before flaming out. The pilot of the other SR-71 is probably scattered somewhere over the Tibet-Nepal border with the wreckage of his airplane."

"As was pointed out already," Torquemada said, "the SR-71 can fly at Mach 3 speed for ninety minutes. Over the Tibet-Nepal border, one SR-71 was shot down by the Soviet MiGs, and Captain Blackwell's airplane flamed out over the Himalayas—"

"Hit a twenty-seven-thousand-foot wall of rock—Mount Makalu," Gabriel said, exhaling smoke, nodding.

"Exactly," Torquemada affirmed, then pointed at the red circle on the map, drawn near the summit of Makalu. "Satellite photos have identified the wreckage at around the twenty-five-thousand-foot mark of Makalu. However, the Sphinx black boxes could be anywhere. They could be lying in the Arun Gorge or spread across the Barun Glacier east of Makalu, for all we really know."

Dillinger whistled, rolling the cigar around in his mouth. "Twenty-five thousand feet of ice and granite. If you people know so much about us, you must also know we're not exactly up for the alpiner-of-the-year award, pal. Speaking for myself, I don't think I'd know the difference between a pi-ton and a ba-ton."

"He's right. We're not mountaineers, we're soldiers for hire, if the cause is right," Gabriel said. "Look, why not go hire yourself an expedition force of Company goons?"

"We want you for this mission," Torquemada said, his voice hard. "We want you to climb the rock and recover the two Sphinx black boxes that recorded the ill-fated mission."

"If those black boxes could be anywhere, hell, this mission could be a wash before we hammer home the first piton," Dillinger pointed out.

"We're hoping they're not just *anywhere*," Torquemada answered.

"A little voice is telling me there's a catch," Gabriel said. "Let's hear it. Why us?"

Folding his hands behind his back, Torquemada began pacing the room. "You're good, Gabriel, even better than when you worked eleventh-hour missions for the CIA. First with your father during the Vietnam War as the father-son team working behind-the-lines suicide missions. Then when you were on your own in Central America, and Western and North Africa. Right now, yes, we do need expendables. We believe that the Soviets will send in a team of gravediggers to sift through the wreckage and recover those Sphinx black boxes. A KGB wet squad, or perhaps even a SPETSNAZ force. It goes without saying that the CIA has blackened Mother Russia's eyes in this, and the Soviets will spare no expense to recover those black boxes. Or spare lives to get them. Should the Soviets recover the Sphinx black boxes, or worse, should one of those pilots still be alive and be captured, Moscow will, without a doubt, finger the United States. Embarrassment over having their airspace so easily violated is probably the only reason the Soviets haven't gone public with this yet. Presently, we have a team encamped at the foothills of Makalu, ten kilometers southwest of a village called Tamerlane. The leader of the Expedition Force Leviathan will alert us the moment the Soviets arrive in Nepal."

"A team?" Boolewarke queried. "Listen, we don't want a bunch of CIA jokers tagging along for the hike, pal."

"He's right. If you've already got this Expedition Force Leviathan there, use them," Gabriel said. "It sounds like you think Ivan might already be there. Put out a call to this Leviathan and get the hunt going. Why wait?"

A thin smile slashed Sprenger's lips as he adjusted his

sunglasses. "The Russians could well already be there. Loaded for bear... or loaded for eagle, so to speak. And besides, our orders are explicit... we want you."

"To do your dirty work, then mysteriously, conveniently disappear afterwards. I get the picture, yeah," Dillinger growled. "Maybe you've already even got four graves dug out in the Arun Gorge, huh?"

Silently, Torquemada and Sprenger stared at Dillinger. The ex-P.I. blew smoke at the operatives.

Gabriel cursed. He was almost afraid to ask his next question, but he had to have his fears confirmed.

"And if you don't get us for the job?"

"Well, let's just say that we have plenty of, uh, dirt on you, Mr. Gabriel," Torquemada said. "You do remember the drug-pusher killings, the private war you launched against the cocaine cartels up and down the East Coast after you discovered your brother died from an overdose? It must've been a very painful time for you, Mr. Gabriel."

The guy was pushing his luck, Gabriel thought. "How can I forget, pal?" the former CIA assassin shot back, feeling the bitter memories slice into his consciousness, the demons of yesterday that lived inside of him and would dance their victory dance in his belly for the rest of his life. "You had one of your ops corner me in Central America about that, too. Said I could work a few assignments for the Company, and in exchange, the CIA would help lead me on to the trail of Saunders. Never panned out. You people didn't have the first clue where Saunders was. But it wasn't the first time you people lied to me." *Probably won't be the last either,* Gabriel thought. Pausing, the ex-CIA assassin read the complete lack of concern on the faces of Torquemada and Sprenger. No, those guys didn't give a damn about anything but getting their way. Somehow, Gabriel couldn't help but feel the CIA was setting them up. Eagle Force had blackened the Company's eyes, too, with their rampage through Tunisia. If the

Company was looking for vengeance, this was the perfect opportunity. Cleaning the table of leftovers or not, Gabriel knew he was always going to be on their hit list to grind up into yesterday's hamburger. And the commandos of Eagle Force, with the possible exception of Boolewarke, were definitely leftovers, scabs that the CIA would like to remove from their side with the knife's edge of treachery.

"So, if we say no, you go public with the Tunisian operation?"

Torquemada stopped in front of Gabriel. "We realize that you think that if you decline you can simply kill us and feed us to the gators. Surely, you know that Langley knows we're here."

"Surely," Dillinger grumbled, the tip of his cigar glowing like an orange eye as he sucked in a lungful of smoke. "Just as surely as I'm thinking about kicking your smug ass, pal."

"If you decline," Sprenger warned, ignoring Dillinger, "there's no telling what Langley will do. Let me put it this way. You walked out on us in Central America to pursue your vendetta against Saunders. The CIA didn't like that. There was a terminate with extreme prejudice mandate on you. Should you and your team successfully complete this mission, meaning recovering the Sphinx black boxes, that mandate will be lifted and your name will be cleared with the Company. Fair enough?"

Gabriel really liked that one. "Even if I do accept, Torquemada," he said, "we work alone. You pull your team out of Nepal or we stay home and watch football this weekend."

"Impossible," Torquemada said.

"Why's that?" Gabriel said gruffly.

"First of all, do any of you speak Nepali, Newari, Bhutia, or Mongol fluently?"

Gabriel felt the frown tugging at the corners of his lips.

Torquemada grinned. "Just what I thought. Secondly, since none of you are mountaineers, you will be getting on-the-job training. You'll learn fast, free of charge. Thirdly, the Sphinx black boxes cannot be tampered with or even moved unless one of our people handles them. Tampering with them, or moving them with anything but the utmost caution, will set off an explosive charge in the boxes. Unless, of course, Captain Blackwell is alive. In that case, the Sphinx black box from his cockpit would already have been deactivated for movement over a period of time. Are you getting the picture now?"

"You act like I've already accepted," Gabriel said, ice in his voice.

"Haven't you?" Sprenger said. Then his expression turned cold. "Or haven't you?"

Gabriel knew the heat was on. If he didn't accept, there was no telling what the CIA would do. He had suspected all along that the CIA had some involvement in the Tunisian contract for slaughter of the Sword of Islam. No, the late Bradley Milton III had not been on his own and had not been all he had seemed. Whatever Milton had been, he was now raven meat in Tunisia. For reasons he would discuss with the other commandos of Eagle Force later, Gabriel decided to go ahead and play the CIA's game. It was a sure bet that if those SR-71s had gone down over the Himalayas, then the Soviets would send in a team of gravediggers. Hunters. Killers, right. And no, they wouldn't let anything short of an invasion of Nepal get in their way of recovering those Sphinx black boxes. If the Soviets did get their hands on those Sphinx black boxes . . . well, Gabriel knew the repercussions would be grim for Uncle Sam. Exactly why the CIA wanted them for the job, he wasn't sure. Hell, he didn't even want to know, even though he suspected what part of their intentions were. Yeah, Eagle Force was getting set up to be shot out of the sky. Most likely there was a real, bona fide mission, all right. But what was at the end of the mission was another matter altogether. Bet your ass, Gabriel decided, he'd be ready to face that music when the time came.

"We're in," Gabriel announced, and saw the shock and anger instantly freeze on the faces of Boolewarke and Dillinger.

"C'mon, Vic," Dillinger growled. "You believe these clowns are leveling with us? Jesus Christ, I never thought I'd see the day when you gave in to the CIA again."

"We're in, and that's final," Gabriel repeated in a stony voice. "And we'll find out if they're leveling with us, Zac, all right? Time unmasks every man."

Dillinger muttered an oath, dropped his cigar, and ground the stogie out on the floor beneath the heel of his combat boot.

"I don't like it either, Vic," Boolewarke declared.

"I'm not asking you to like it, Dutch." Gabriel asked Torquemada, "What about transportation?"

"A C-130 Hercules is fueled and can be ready to fly out at any time." Torquemada checked his Seiko. "We'd like you ready to go at twenty-four hundred hours. Definitely no later than oh two hundred. Arrangements will be made to pick you and your men up and move you from here to the departure site. Is that a problem?"

"We pick our own weapons before leaving," Gabriel said.

"Fine," Sprenger agreed. "Then you do acknowledge that you will be working in conjunction with Expedition Force Leviathan?"

"Acknowledged but disagreed on," Gabriel said, a steely edge to his voice. "I don't like having my every move monitored by CIA killers."

"Two operatives, that's all," Torquemada said. "They know the language, the country, and they are expert mountain climbers. The rest of the force is made up of

Sherpas who will act as guides and porters, not monitors. You will be in excellent hands."

"That's what we're afraid of," Dillinger grumbled.

And the ex-P.I. echoed Gabriel's feelings exactly.

"You have nothing to fear," Sprenger said, an odd smile dancing over his lips, "but yourselves. Nothing at all to fear but the darkness in your own hearts."

"Christ," Dillinger growled, and looked at Gabriel, "where the fuck does the CIA dig these guys up?"

"What about pay?" Gabriel asked.

Torquemada looked astonished. "Pay? My dear Mr. Gabriel, you're doing this for love of country. Put your mercenary selves aside, soldiers. Do something in the patriotic spirit . . . for once. This one's for Uncle Sam."

"I thought I heard the word *hire* repeatedly?" Gabriel said. "I thought when you hired somebody that meant payment for services rendered."

"We're not authorized to offer you money," Torquemada said. "Besides . . . you netted a pretty good haul from the late Bradley Milton III anyway, didn't you?"

Angrily, Dillinger looked at Gabriel, the ex-P.I. jerking a thumb at Torquemada. "Get this son of a bitch outta my sight before I send him back to Langley . . . wrapped up in the Stars and Stripes with his nutbag crammed in his big mouth."

Gabriel clenched his jaw. Those were his sentiments, too. Exactly. Damn right.

"How come I'm getting this creepy kind of feeling walking all up and down my back when you talk? How come I'm getting this kind of almost nauseating tightness in my guts that's warning me you're a goddamn liar? Why don't you explain that to me, mister, huh? If you can. If you will. You brought him back, but you didn't bring him back. You brought the shipment back, but you didn't bring the shipment back. I'm hearing bullshit, mister, and I don't like it."

Vic Gabriel bit down on a rage that was mounting in his heart and threatening to blow his blood pressure right out his eardrums. Try as he might to swallow that rage, he couldn't. He was a human time bomb sitting right on top of a rumbling volcano. Clearing his throat, Gabriel stood, a bone in his knee cracking. He fished a rumpled pack of Marlboros out of his green-camoued fatigues, torched the deathstick with a flick of his Zippo. A stainless steel Detonics .45 Combat Master Mark VI was riding heavy on his hip. He felt a twitching sensation run down his arm, a current of electricity filtering through his gunhand. At the moment, he didn't dare look the CIA paramilitary operatives in the eye. No, he decided, he would just let the mystery unfold. Slowly. Right before their eyes. Walk them right into it. Throw them as much deceit and denial as they had shown him. No. He corrected himself. They had shown him nothing. But he had discovered everything. Did they know that he now knew? And if they did know that he knew, what were they planning to do about it?

He heard those grim questions rattling around in his mind, over and over. Like broken bones. He had done the CIA's bidding, and he felt as if he had sold his soul to the devil. Now he was standing, alone with the devil. He had been their unwitting tool. At least that had been so in the beginning. Once their denial began to unravel before his eyes, he had become a skeleton, fumbling around in the dark, looking for the key. Well, he had found that key, and he was about to open the door.

"You know," Gabriel began, hard gaze fixed on dark-green canvas, the cawing of exotic birds and the chirping of insects filtering down around the large tent, as if the Nicaraguan jungle was closing in on them, a predatory beast about to swallow the CIA Command HQ whole, "it's like I've been staring into a mirror for years and years, only I wasn't there, like I was invisible. I went along with all the bullshit because I was one of you, or at least a part

of you, even though I didn't really want to be a part of you. I stumbled into this whole game because I needed you. I learned the game quick, learned it in Nam actually, hell, even felt like I invented a few new twists to the game myself along the way. I learned, the hardest way possible. I learned when my father was murdered in Paris. I learned even more after my brother died from a fatal overdose. I learned from all those mistakes, mistakes that were created both internally and externally. Within and without. The within me couldn't leave the without alone. I kept making the same mistakes, even though I knew better. And because I knew better, I hold myself more accountable than someone who plain old just doesn't give a shit.

"Yeah, I kept staring and staring into that mirror, all right, but all I could see was shadow and glass. It all eluded me, because it was all an illusion. And the illusion had lured me in, lured me in good and locked me up, because I wanted to patch everything up my way, quick and clean, but there's no quick and clean about it. That's what illusion is. Illusion is evil. Evil is an illusion. Why, you might ask? Because it always looks good in the beginning, that's why. But the beautiful woman always turns into an old, ugly hag real soon. You see her in the distance, a real beautiful woman, the most beautiful woman you've ever seen. She calls you, wants you, she's seducing you. You're walking through a fog because your desire for her overpowers you, and the fog is your desire and it grows thicker the closer you get to her. When that fog finally clears, she's still there, you're right up on her, staring into her eyes, leaning down to kiss her. Suddenly, something isn't right, there's a change, something you can feel in the air but can't put a finger on. You're ready for her, but right before your eyes the old hag is grinning up at you. And there's maggots spewing out of her mouth. Maggots and puke and shit. Of course, by then, it's too late. She's dug her claws into your face and won't let you

go and you're screaming in fear because you know you're a
dead man. She's pumping into your mouth all of what
your desire really is. And it's too late. Usually."

"What the hell are you talking about, mister? You're
rambling. I'm hearing more bullshit on top of more bullshit.
Now, I want some fucking answers out of you, not a bunch
of goddamn riddles or some twisted fairy tale out of your
sick fuckin' mind. I want answers, not riddles. Truth, not
lies. Am I getting through to you?"

"Loud and clear, Colonel. You've gotten through, all
right. You see . . . for so long I was always, uh, comfortably
numb to all of it. We were the good guys," Gabriel said,
and blew a cloud of smoke at the canvas wall. Turning, he
stared for a moment at the bright-orange fingers of sunlight that knifed through the tent flaps. "And they were the
bad guys. I'm no longer comfortably numb. I'm very, very
uncomfortably numb. And I feel very, very old all of a
sudden. And very, very fucking mean."

"I don't give a damn what you're feeling, mister. We
had a deal. We expect you to deliver. I want delivery.
Now!"

Blowing a stream of smoke, Gabriel dropped the butt
on the dirt floor, ground it beneath the bootheel of a black
combat boot. Steel in his eyes, he turned and looked at
them. The stink of sweat pierced into his nose. A ball of
moisture broke from his brow, burned into his eye.

There were three of them. Ex-Army colonel Ben
Nelson stood, several inches over six feet tall. His hands
on his hips, he was staring at Gabriel with dark accusa-
tion in his gray eyes. Nelson was a lean, broad-shouldered
man with a square face and a jutting jaw. He was the man
in the forefront of the denial, Gabriel knew. The other two
shadows in the game were typical paramilitary operatives
dredged up by the CIA's Special Operations Division,
Cronin and Steele. Typical, because they were the hired
animals from SOD. Cold. Brutal. Treacherous. Loyal to

*nothing and no one except themselves and blood money.
They were vultures, circling over the carnage, waiting to
claim their chunk of the spoils. Cronin and Steele, both
ops tall and lean, their sunburned, sweaty faces carved in
granite death's-heads expressions just like Nelson's grim
features, wore .45 Colt ACPs, holstered on their hips.
Nelson, for reasons Gabriel could only begin to guess,
opted for the decimating firepower of a stainless steel .44
AutoMag.*

"We had a deal, all right, Colonel," Gabriel said.
"Roberto Alvarez, for one Michael Saunders, the killer of
my father."

Nelson heaved a sigh. "I'm getting real exasperated
with you, mister. Real quick. That has a way of making me
feel real mean, real quick. And my mean may just be a
little more ugly than yours. Let's get that shit straightened
out right now.

"Okay. Now let's try to see why we're having this
classic failure to communicate here. You radioed in with
your team, twenty klicks outside of Managua, two days
ago. You were picked up two hours after you radioed for e
and e by our chopper team. You had the shipment and you
had Alvarez, so you said. Now, it doesn't take two whole
fucking days to fly a hundred klicks from where you were
picked up. You made no radio contact after that initial
transmission. Bottom line—you left us in the dark, wondering
just what the hell was going down. Now, you tell me just
what am I supposed to think?"

"Whoa," Gabriel said, lifting his hand for a moment.
"Let's back up here. I was told to seize this shipment of
Soviet RPG-7s and other crates of Soviet hardware from
Alvarez, because Alvarez was throwing a real monkey
wrench into Company operations down here. He was a key
guerrilla leader and he was pissing all over the Company's
parade of contras. I was told to abduct Alvarez and bring
him back to you for interrogation. I was also told by you

that I would be contacted at the LZ by your man, who would then relay solid intel to me about Saunders's whereabouts. The man never showed. That's my bottom line, Colonel. I was left in the dark."

Nelson clenched his jaw, turned away from Gabriel, and began pacing back and forth in front of Cronin and Steele.

"I explained that."

"You explained that my contact was shot and killed. By who and for what reason, I still don't know."

Nelson gritted his teeth. "You either got shit in your ears or shit for brains. There's a fuckin' war going on in this country, mister. People die during wars, or haven't you noticed that? Your man was killed when guerrilla rebels overran his camp. They were apparently outnumbered pretty fuckin' good, butchered in their sleep before they even knew what was hitting them. The sonsofbitches even stripped the skin right off their bones with machetes, didn't leave nothin' but a pool of guts for some starving spic peasant."

Gabriel nodded. "Sounds good, kinda. Yeah, Colonel, I heard all that. I heard that, and I wonder, wonder, wonder."

Cronin spoke up. "Wonder what? You calling the Colonel a liar?"

Nelson ignored Cronin. "Listen, asshole, you got that shipment or not? Have you got Alvarez or not?"

"I've got both."

"All right, then. That's what I want to hear. I want it straight up. Is the shipment in one piece?"

"One piece, safe and sound, yeah. Five crates, like you said. Personally, I found it hard to believe that five crates that size would be that important to you."

"You're here to follow orders, mister, not speculate and make half-assed assumptions."

"*I know. I lived up to my end of the deal. In fact, you could say I died up to my end of the deal.*"

Nelson peered at Gabriel. "*You brought Alvarez?*"

Gabriel nodded.

"*Alive?*"

"*As alive as he'll ever be.*"

"*What's that supposed to mean?*"

"*It's all part of being comfortably numb, Colonel. Why don't you come and see for yourself.*"

Nelson clenched his jaw, jerked a sideways nod. "*Move out.*"

Slowly, Vic Gabriel walked toward the tent flaps. The moment of truth, he knew, would arrive. Soon enough. The key was in his hand.

And the door was creaking open.

Whatever was beyond that door awaited the masters of deceit and denial.

Chapter 5

A rumble broke across the black sky. The Sherpa youth froze in his tracks. *What are the mountain gods so angry about?*

Ang Karzim Bhantaj stepped away from his family's yurt. The bitter cold seemed to saw right through his fur-and-leather garments like the gnawing teeth of a predatory animal. Not even the thick yak hide could combat such a fierce chill, but he realized his discomfort was caused by more than just the icy winds that were breathed down from the mountains by the ancient gods. Fear. Yes, he was indeed afraid. What caused the tightening of his chest and throat, though, he was not certain. He had a feeling, though, deep in his gut, that a bad fate was going to be visited upon the village. Shivering, standing in a foot of snow, *Ang* Karzim Bhantaj searched the night, listened as the rumble grew into a sound like rolling thunder.

Avalanche.

Perhaps, *Ang* Bhantaj thought, the yeti and his lady were angry, too, and he tugged his bow higher up on his shoulder, ready to slide an arrow from his leather quiver, worried that some evil creature might step out of the dark shadows of the night and attack him. For days now, the thunder had sounded from the Great Wall of Ice. Its jagged peaks veiled by clouds, the Snowy Range loomed into the blackness of a sky that seemed to sit right on top of the earth, the towering walls of snow-blanketed rock washed over in a dull white sheen by the light of a full moon. A heavy carpet of snow had already fallen over the mountains, much earlier this season than usual. Another omen? The Sherpa youth could not shake off the fear.

The ground beneath *Ang* Bhantaj kept trembling, and for a brief second the son of the village khan wondered if the earth might open up against the crushing weight of the avalanche and swallow the village whole. He could only hope that the main tongue of the avalanche did not descend right on top of his village. The yurts, tents made of felt and yak hide stretched over sturdy wooden frames, would be pulped beneath an avalanche. His village, sitting near the foothills of Mount Makalu, had been pounded by an avalanche before. Many had died. Many had lost their homes. Death was not a stranger to the villagers of Tamerlane. If they were afraid, then the villagers did not acknowledge their fear, for no one ventured forth from their yurts, as the mountain gods roared and roared from their lofty throne.

Something bad had already happened on the mountain, Bhantaj knew, and even the yak herds were restless, appeared frightened. For days and nights now the mountain and the valley had been swarmed over by the giant metallic birds he believed were called airplanes. Some of the larger metallic birds thundered across the skies, while the smaller of the winged demons shrieked over the village. They had stayed high above the mountains, hugging, it seemed, the sky itself as they soared over the valley. Had they been watching the village? Bhantaj wondered. What did they want? Because of the sky dwellers, would the yeti and his lady become violently angered that their home was being spied on? Worse still, it had been told to him by the villagers that a team of foreigners and a band of Sherpa guides and porters had gone up the mountain. That journey began many weeks ago. More strangers, he thought, who had gone to the mountain and invaded the home of the gods and the yeti. In search of glory, they had most likely, it was said, been defeated in death by the evil spirits who dwelled on the mountain. It was a bad sign of things to come, he believed.

Suddenly, the roar ended. A hollow silence seemed to echo down from the throne of the gods and cloak Tamerlane in a sigh. And *Ang* Bhantaj listened to the night. The silence was good. There was peace in the silence, and there was peace now in his spirit. The avalanche would not come crushing down on the village, after all. At least, not this time.

Then he heard it. Another faint rumble that grew into an ominous roar. Then the rolling thunder was right above young Bhantaj. He looked up, scouring the black veil of the starlit heavens above. Peering skyward through hooded eyelids, he barely made out the shapes of the giant metallic birds. There were three of the birds, rumbling, descending low over the valley. Then he spotted the dark shadows as they jumped from the bellies of those birds. Alarmed, he ran into the yurt, woke his father. Together, they went outside. *Noyans* and *bahadurs,* the men of the village who were the strongest warriors and hunters, rushed outside their yurts. They, too, watched the sky, pointing at the black shapes falling to the earth, and *Ang* Bhantaj read the fear in their eyes. Even the yaks stirred from sleep, began milling around the yurts, as if they could sense the growing anxiety of their masters.

Moments later, the descending figures turned into the dark shadows of men. Twenty, thirty, perhaps forty shadows as those men hit the snow, as silent as a stalking snow leopard, rolling on their sides, the great black sheets tied to their backs billowing behind them.

And *Ang* Bhantaj reached into his quiver for an arrow. Those men had guns, and even as they came out of their rolls on the ground, they were swinging their weapons toward the warriors of Tamerlane. Those weapons blazed orange flame, and *Ang* Bhantaj saw two of his people tumble to the ground, great spurts of blood erupting from their chests. The invaders were dropping all around the village, scattering, surging in on the yurts. They were foreigners.

"*Stoi! Stoi! Vigivres! Vigivres!*" they barked.

Ang Bhantaj recognized the foreign tongue.

The invaders were Russian.

Shouting and cursing ringing in his ears, barely aware of the yaks stampeding beyond the yurts, Bhantaj felt the fear root him to the ground, watched as the Russians swarmed around Tamerlane like wild beasts.

"Sphinx black boxes?" Hands folded in his lap, Johnny Simms shook his head. "Man, what in the world have you gotten us into, Victor?"

"A Nepali killhunt, wrapped in a real riddle, my friend, that's what," Henry van Boolewarke said.

The rumble of the C-130's propjet engines beginning to buzzsaw through his head after twelve hours of flight, Vic Gabriel poured himself another cup of black coffee from his thermos. Johnny Simms had asked the same question twice during the past hour. A question, Gabriel admitted to himself, that he didn't have a ready answer for. Boolewarke, Gabriel mused, just came about as close to an answer as any of them would get. In the long run that riddle, though, would be solved. One way or another. And the blood would run, Gabriel suspected. Run cold down the icy slopes of Makalu.

Standing, Gabriel fished a Marlboro out of a rumpled pack, flicked his Zippo, and torched up the smoke. Drawing deep on his smoke, Gabriel began pacing in front of his commandos. The other three commandos of Eagle Force sat on a bench in the aft section of the fixed-wing gunship, smoking, sipping coffee. Judging by their solemn expressions, Gabriel knew each commando was silently hashing over the mission, mentally gauging a number of possibilities, asking themselves questions. And yeah, wondering what grim fate might be waiting for them in Nepal.

The CIA appeared deadly serious about recovering the Sphinx black boxes. A C-130 gunship, armed with 7.62mm Vulcan miniguns and 40mm Bofors and 20mm Gatling cannons, wasn't just a bird you took out for a recon mission, Gabriel knew. No, the warning bells in Gabriel's head wouldn't go silent anytime soon. Past experience with Company treachery wouldn't allow Gabriel to drop his guard for a second.

Not with CIA assassins hanging around.

Up front, close to the cockpit door, an operative, code-named Attila, was standing behind another operative who stayed glued to a large radio console. Except for an armor-plated, military jeep with a mounted .50-caliber machine gun in the canvas-covered bed and three 15-gallon drums of gasoline beside that jeep, the cargo hold was empty. The small arms Eagle Force would tote up Mount Makalu were stored in a metal bin on the forward portside of the fuselage. After they hit the LZ by parachute, that bin would be emptied of three HK33 assault rifles and spare clips, one 7.62mm NATO M60 machine gun, an MM1 multiround projectile launcher, and three dozen fragmentation and thermite grenades. The M60 was requested by Boolewarke, who kept his favored Barnett Panzer crossbow and black leather quiver, stuffed with arrows, by his side. The Dutchman hated anything that even smelled of KGB or SPETSNAZ because of the insidious web of violence and mayhem the Russian armed forces and their cronies had woven around South Africa. And Gabriel knew the Afrikaner's remembrance of his brutal experience in Angola, where Boolewarke had almost gotten killed by SPETSNAZ, wouldn't do anything to cool the Dutchman's fever and lust to spill Russian blood. Now with the possibility of either SPETSNAZ or a KGB murder squad showing up at the end of the line in Nepal, Gabriel knew Dutch was anxious to belt that M60 and let it rip. And Dutch had already voiced his hope for the best—or the worst—*depending upon how many Russians showed up on Mount Makalu*. Even though Boolewarke was eager for battle against Russian hitters, Gabriel was keeping his fingers crossed that this would be nothing more than a recovery mission. There was no question in Gabriel's mind or the minds of his commandos about his courage. But Gabriel didn't need to be looking over his shoulder for both Ivan—and CIA assassins on a killhunt with orders to purge him of past sins the Company felt he had committed against them. Scaling Mount Makalu in search of the Sphinx black boxes was going to be grim chore enough. No matter what, though, Eagle Force had to be prepared for any possibility. There was a good chance, Gabriel knew, that the enemy could turn out to be anybody, and *everybody* on this mission. Eagle Force stood alone, as far as Gabriel was concerned. The ex–Special Forces warrior knew his commandos felt likewise.

At the moment, all four Eagle Force commandos were outfitted with USMC Ka-Bar fighting knives and garrotes. With his passionate admiration for the late great general George Patton, Dillinger didn't go anywhere without his pearl-handled .45 Colt automatics. Gabriel, Simms, and Boolewarke carried stainless steel .44 Ruger Redhawk Magnums in hip holsters, the walnut butts jutting forward for a crossdraw. Hand-held cannons, the Ruger Redhawk would tunnel out wound channels in a target the size of a grapefruit.

There was something else Gabriel had added to their garb. Whether they were togged in combat black, or eventually donning whitesuit for the ascent up Makalu, each commando would wear a patch of an eagle with its wings spread on his right shoulder. From there on, the

American bald eagle would be their trademark. Patriotism. Team spirit. An identifying bond of loyalty and commitment to each other.

Zac Dillinger, his brow furrowed in pensive thought, was chomping around a fat stogie, thick plumes of cigar smoke wreathing around the ex-P.I.'s grizzled face. "Whatever we've gotten ourselves into, Johnny Boy, you can bet your ass it won't be good."

"We?" Boolewarke said gruffly. "As I recall, chum, *we* is you and your buddy, Simms, thanks to your little Mafia hunting excursion."

Gabriel saw the storm set in the eyes of Simms and Dillinger. As an ex-Recces commando, Boolewarke had some strong, and most likely, Gabriel suspected, some torn and troubled views about apartheid. White mercs in general, and South African soldiers in particular, believed, or wanted to believe, Gabriel knew from his time as a dog of war in Southwest Africa, that the black man lacked the heart and skill to be a competent professional soldier. Gabriel didn't believe that for a second, had seen that myth shot down firsthand by more than one black soldier or commando. As for Johnny Simms, well, time and again, in Central America then during the first Eagle Force mission, Gabriel recalled, Simms had proven himself tough, reliable, loyal, and unflinching in the eye of a firefight. And Gabriel knew that Johnny Simms was aware that Henry van Boolewarke had some definite opinions about the explosive racial situation in South Africa. But Boolewarke, Gabriel believed, was a far cry from being a hard-hearted racist; it just didn't seem to be part of the man's character. Even though Simms and Boolewarke had opposing views about the RSA, Gabriel hadn't seen or heard either man throw his opinions in the face of the other man to the point of igniting violent confrontation. Having displayed deadly martial skill during the first mission, both men realized that action does, indeed, speak louder, much louder, than words. Still, a close-knit friendship, Gabriel thought, wasn't on the horizon between Simms and Boolewarke. As commandos of Eagle Force, they both knew they were soldiers with a mission, men fighting for whatever cause, in the name of justice, called them. Trust and respect had to be a ruling force among the commandos of Eagle Force. Trust and respect beefed up the chances for their survival together as a team. It was that simple. And they had earned trust and respect from each other in the killing fields of Tunisia.

"All right, all right," Gabriel growled, raking a hard stare over his troops. "Let's not fall into a bunch of petty bickering among ourselves like we're some fucking high school debutantes. I don't care if this whole thing started in a goddamn titty bar in Miami or not. The fact is, the goons at Langley most likely would've found us anyway for this big special recovery mission of theirs."

"So they blackmail us into doin' a job for them," Simms said. "No tellin' what else they got in mind in their bag of dirty tricks, Vic. We ain't exactly the CIA's fair-haired boys, y'know. We each got a past with them that they'd like to erase with a quick subgun burst. Shit, this whole thing stinks of a setup. Just look at that dude," the black commando said, nodding toward the operative Attila. "If he ain't got the look of trouble about him, if he ain't a killer with word from SOD to tag our asses, I'll give Dutchie here my cut from the last mission."

"I accept," Boolewarke said, cocking a wry grin at Simms, then winking at Gabriel. "Provided we even make it up and back down that mountain," he added, grim, tight-lipped.

"Which brings us to another problem," Dillinger said, and blew a cloud of cigar smoke toward the ceiling. "We don't know the first thing about mountaineering, much less scaling a rock like Makalu. A sheet of snow and ice that's killed a lot of men who *did know* what the hell they were doing."

Gabriel couldn't suppress a half-grin as he took a deep drag on his cigarette. "I heard something once about there not being problems . . ."

"Only solutions, yeah, yeah, right," Dillinger growled, frowning. "We already know we're getting on-the-job training. I suppose there's our solution."

"Training, right, at our expense," Simms added. "Some solution."

"Well, I *do* have some climbing experience," Gabriel informed the commandos.

And he did. As a boy living in the Colorado Rockies with his father and brother, the three of them would often set out to scale a particularly difficult cliff. There was no question about it—all of them were stepping onto very unfamiliar turf. Even though he had some experience with mountain climbing under his belt, Gabriel knew he wasn't exactly one hundred percent capable of scaling a 27,000-foot wall of rock. Rock that could cripple a man with one false slip on a jagged edge of icy rock. Rock that could hurl a careless man off the face of the mountain and send him plunging into oblivion. Vic Gabriel had every right to be worried about this outing, and he began to think he must've been crazy for accepting the CIA's mission in the first place. Then he remembered something his father had once told him before setting out on a mountaineering venture.

The only obstacle a man ever really faces, Son, is himself. The only obstacle is in your mind. A man's strength, Vic, is not in the size of his muscles, but in the size of his heart. I believe every man is born with a certain degree of courage. Courage itself is inherent for the sheer necessity of survival. Heart, on the other hand, is found inside yourself, and it will grow only if you keep on trying. Outside of a life-threatening situation, it doesn't matter so much if you fail at something. The true test of character is how a man reacts to failure. Failure can be a good thing, but only if you keep trying harder, much harder than before. Try until you succeed. And never, never rest on success. A man can often steal success from himself through complacency.

"So, where's that leave us?" Simms asked.

Gabriel dropped his smoke to the floorboard, crushed the butt beneath the heel of his combat boot. "With a lot of heart, Johnny... I hope. There's no doubt we'll be facing off with somebody. Either Ivan or the Company, or both, I don't know—yet. Personally, I hope the CIA does come after us, but they'll most likely do it after we've recovered the Sphinx black boxes. That way, we can wash our hands of them for good. So let's tentatively call this Operation Pontius Pilate," he cracked, though he felt anything but humorous.

"I still don't buy that crap about us being good and that's why they wanted us for this mission," Dillinger said, flicking a thick wad of ashes on the floor.

"They'll try and sell you some shit, all right. I've been there and back before with them," Gabriel said. "Smeared in their shit, from head to toe."

"What? Damn!"

Even through the rumble of the propjet engines, Gabriel made out the voice of anger and worry. Looking forward, he saw Attila heading toward them suddenly.

"Uh-oh. Now what?" Simms wondered aloud. "Attila the Hun there looks a little worried, if you ask me."

"Is there a problem back here?" Attila asked, stopping and facing the commandos of Eagle Force.

"Yeah," Johnny Simms answered.

"The problem just asked if there's a problem," Dillinger finished, blowing smoke at the operative, grinning at his own wisecrack.

Gaze narrowed, Gabriel looked at Attila. There was

assassin written all over the operative, Gabriel concluded. Hell, he knew the look. He wore it himself. The coldness in the eyes. The black halo of invincibility a man who'd been to hell and back wore. The loose, confident, almost arrogant way a man carried himself, even though the constant tension was right there in the face and eyes. Attila was a big guy, topping six foot and two hundred pounds of solid muscle. Attila could hold his own in a toe-to-toe headknocker, Gabriel was sure. The Company operative, who had taken the name of the greatest of Huns, had green eyes—gimlets, Gabriel thought, that bored through a man in an attempt to search the soul for any dark secrets. Attila was one tough nut, Gabriel decided. *But every man has a crack that can be broken wide, if you look hard enough*, Gabriel thought. *A fissure in his character just waiting to open up and swallow him alive.*

Togged in black camos and combat boots, Attila rested his hands on his hips. "Just what I need on my hands— four bad comedians who want to play tough guy."

"Who's playing?" Boolewarke growled.

"Your hands?" Simms queried. "Somebody die and leave you in charge? I thought our man here," he said, glancing at Gabriel, "was running the show?"

"You thought wrong, soldier," Attila shot back. "And you can do yourself, me, and your buddies a big favor from here on out. One that might get you home alive."

"Yeah? What's that?" Simms asked, ice in his voice.

"Let me do the thinking."

Great, thought Gabriel. *Then we might all end up blocks of human ice on the slopes of Makalu.*

Before setting out on the mission, Gabriel suspected he'd be playing the role of subordinate to the CIA assassins. Attila could throw his weight around, but as the man who had tracked Dillinger, Simms, and Boolewarke down in the genesis of Eagle Force, Gabriel knew the three commandos would look to him for leadership. Gabriel's leadership role was silently acknowledged by the other three commandos, but he knew he'd never have to point out the fact that, yeah, he was the Man. He'd earned the right through blood passage and baptism in hellfire. And earned the right through trust and respect. Each man of Eagle Force was an individual in his own right, and that was part of their strength. They were also a nucleus, a four-man unit that could roll onto the killing fields as one body, a juggernaut of death and destruction.

"All right, I want that jeep rolled up onto landing skids," Attila said. "When we hit the ground, we've gotta head west. There's been a change of plans."

Gabriel didn't like the sound of that. "What change?"

"We've got to go to Kathmandu first to link up with Expedition Force Leviathan."

"Why?" Gabriel growled as Attila paused, obviously wanting somebody to fish information out of him. The guy was going to play the role for all he was worth, Gabriel thought. *The son of a bitch is going for an Oscar.*

Attila was grim. "The Russians have arrived in Nepal. A lot of Russians, I might add."

A half-smile ghosted the Dutchman's lips.

Russians, Gabriel thought. SPETSNAZ or KGB? Hell, it didn't really matter, he decided. Whomever Moscow had sent, Vic Gabriel definitely knew the blood would run now. Run cold. Run like a river down the icy slopes of Makalu.

Nepal was about to be visited by Death. Invaded by Destruction and Mayhem.

Vic Gabriel sucked in a deep breath through his nose, an iceball of tension lodging in his guts.

"What in the hell!"
Vic Gabriel felt a healthy kind of tension warm but steel his guts as he watched, from the backseat of the jeep, the ugly tension that twisted Colonel Nelson's face, tightened

*the CIA man's mouthline into confusion and anger. Healthy
tension, Vic Gabriel knew, because he had been blessed by
his father's wisdom while schooled in a basic philosophy, a
simple way of living that allowed a man to be humble but
strong. He remembered his father's words at that moment
as the jeep cut a swath through a ring of mahogany trees
and began surging across the grass plain.*

When a man learns the difference between right and
wrong, accepts that there is right and wrong and lives by a
code of honor and respect for life, he can then walk with
his head up, look anyone in the eye. Because his heart
tells him he is right and he knows he is living right and
willing to continue to live that way, he doesn't have to walk
in fear and deception. This is example by character, Son,
without having to make an issue of it, without having to
say, "Look at me, I'm better than you, why can't you be
like this, too?" When you live right, you carry your own
weight. But be careful of those living in fear and deceit.
They are the weak, letting themselves be overpowered by
their desires, feeding their own grandiosity by living the
illusion, indeed, lusting after the illusion. Be careful of the
fearful and the deceitful. They will want to drag you down.
You will find that sometimes you will have to carry the
burden of those who wish to drag you down. Remember,
you can only do so much for them. Unless they are willing
to see themselves as they really are, they will perish.
Quickly, but not quietly. Just look at history. Look at the
Hitlers, the Napoleons, the Stalins, all the great tyrants
and dictators. What they cannot control, they have to
destroy. What they cannot conquer, they have to kill. In
the end, they realized that they were never in control,
because they were never in control of themselves. So they
had to destroy themselves and all that they had created.
Destroy themselves and all that they had created and
never understand or confess as to why they felt compelled
to do so. They had reached this point because at some

point in time, they became their own God. Live by a code of honor and a respect for life, Son, and be willing to go to any lengths to do this. When a man or a woman can come to a no-bullshit terms with this, then he no longer has to fear tomorrow. Or himself. Or anyone else.

As his father's voice faded from his mind, Vic Gabriel returned to the no-bullshit terms of the present.

"What in the fucking hell's goin' on here!"

Nelson's voice reached new heights of simmering rage. With dark sunglasses shielding his eyes from the harsh glare of the high-noon sun, it was difficult for Gabriel to read into the man's head. But Vic Gabriel had the guy staked out already, so he fixed steely attention on the destruction and carnage ahead.

A twisting pall of black smoke rose from one of the two Huey gunships. Flames licked away from the fuselage, and three corpses lay just beyond the reach of the crackling fire, mangled bodies facedown in crimson pools.

Instantly as Cronin braked the jeep near the second Huey, the chopper undamaged but eerily planted on the plain in silent stillness, the three paramilitary operatives snatched up M-16s, hopped out.

"Guerrillas?" *Vic Gabriel posed, and heard his hollow question fall on deaf ears.*

Cronin and Steele jumped up into the fuselage of the silent gunship. The chain of low-lying hills to the north became like some blurry lump, a ghostly wave of giant tombstones in Gabriel's sight as he followed the ops into the fuselage.

Cronin burst out of the cockpit. "Dead. Both of them. Shot in the face, point-blank. Guns are on the floor like they were reaching. . . ."

Steele strode to the aft of the gunship. There, five large crates sat on the floorboard. The lid on one of the crates was cracked open. And a blood-slickened arm dangled down the side of that crate.

Nelson bared his teeth in savage fury. "Or like they suddenly figured out what was going down."

Vic Gabriel stopped cold in his tracks between Cronin and Nelson. He felt their eyes crawling over him. Suddenly he knew he was standing, naked, alone in the icy glare of the ugly truth. And the glare of that truth blinded the CIA mercenaries for a split second.

Long enough for Gabriel to snake his Detonics .45 from his holster.

Steele swung his M-16 toward Gabriel. Vic Gabriel pumped one .45 slug into Steele's face. As Steele slammed off the bulkhead, Gabriel wheeled, drilled another bone-crusher into Cronin's chest, flinging him into the cockpit.

Nelson's .44 AutoMag was drawn and tracking. Nelson triggered the cannon, but Gabriel launched himself sideways. As the .44 slug thudded into a crate, Gabriel spun out of his roll.

It was over with in less time than it takes to blink an eye.

Hitting a combat crouch, Gabriel triggered the Detonics .45 twice. The first slug punched into Nelson's shoulder. Screaming, the AutoMag spinning away from him, Nelson hammered off the cockpit doorway. Gabriel slapped some bloody insurance on that first round, driving another slug into Nelson's gunarm, the colonel's sunglasses flying away from his face as he snapped his head sideways in excruciating agony.

Clutching his shattered arm, eyelids slitted, lips twisted, Nelson squirmed to sit up and brace his back against the bulkhead. "Y-you bastard . . ."

Steely gaze leveled on Nelson, Gabriel backed up. Gun trained on the CIA man, Gabriel threw the lid open. He stepped aside to give Nelson a full view of the corpse.

"Al-Alvarez . . ."

Vic Gabriel let the shock soak in. An empty stare from the dead man's eyes seemed to focus on Nelson. A gaping

*black slit still oozed trickles of blood from where Gabriel
had drawn a machete across the dead man's throat.*

*And Roberto Alvarez was outstretched atop a stack of
white bricks. Dead as shit, having already spewed out a
great gush of blood over his white gold. No. White poison.*

*"I figure there's maybe three to four hundred kilos of
White Lady in these crates, Colonel."*

*Vic Gabriel's voice seemed to hang in the fuselage.
Except for the crackle of nearby flames, there was heavy
silence in the gunship.*

*"High-grade," Gabriel went on. "Highest grade of
pure Snow White going."*

*Fear shadowed Nelson's face. "W-wait a minute . . . you
don't understand . . ."*

*"I understand perfectly, Colonel. Does the free world
need your contras to win this badly? You think this is
going to save Latin America? I understand, all right. And
so it goes. On and on."*

"Listen to me, goddammit!"

*Vic Gabriel felt his finger tighten around the trigger
of his Detonics .45. A death's-head grin twisted his lips.
He looked down at Nelson and said, "On and on. The
grandiose march to their graves. They look down at the
shadow and glass. They look down into the abyss, and
they scream. And, Colonel . . . let there be darkness."*

Chapter 6

Lieutenant General Mikhail Vishtka had worked him-self up into a rage. A killing rage. He had been assigned a grim task by the VGK, the Soviet Supreme High Com-mand, and he was worried. Should he return to Moskva without evidence of the CIA reconnaissance planes, which had nearly wiped out a strategic satellite defense base near the Chinese border in a treacherous attack, he might as well pack his belongings and board the next train bound for Siberia. Then there was the possibility he would just be shot in the head, right behind the ear. And the customary execution of a traitor or a failure to the mother-land required that the bullet be provided by a member of his family. First disgrace, then death or exile. That was the price for failure in the line of duty. There were no choices. There were no options.

As commander of the elite SPETSNAZ Airborne Moun-tain Task Force *Krasnaya Zvezda*—Red Star—the lieuten-ant general knew his first task was to break the will of the Tamerlane villagers. Submission to his authority meant controlling the Sherpas. Controlling the Sherpas meant he would weed out any dangerous individuals. With brutality, he intended to do just that. Quickly.

A man who had learned his lessons well from harsh personal experience, Vishtka had survived both the Nazis and Stalin. He had known terror, and he knew the power of terror. Terror was simply a tool, *nyet*, terror was a weapon to be used, he believed. And he was in the mood to use just such a weapon. He had to.

For long moments, his gloved hands clasped behind his back, Vishtka paced in front of the captive Sherpas. Like cattle, they had been rounded up by AK-47–wielding SPETSNAZ commandos in whitesuit and lined up in front of their yurts. Sherpa men, women, and children, stripped down to undergarments of silk, stood now, shivering in the cold. If they were afraid, then they did not show their fear. Instead, Vishtka found himself staring at the face of hatred and defiance. Both young and old, both man and woman, looked at Vishtka with utter contempt. The lieutenant general felt his blood run hot with fury, even as icy blasts of wind ripped down from the Makalu massif. Sherpas. Mongols. Both were of the same Asian bloodline, Vishtka thought. The ancestors of the Tamerlane villagers, the evil Tartars, he knew, had ravaged Mother Russia during the thirteenth century. The plague of the Golden Horde. The scourge of the Mongol yoke. Indeed, there was even some Mongol blood in his own village along the Dnieper. He cringed at the mere thought of the poison that might be in his blood. More than seven centuries ago, the son of Genghis Khan, Jochi, and his Golden Horde, it was told by the village elders, who had had the terrible legends passed on to them by the previous generation, had laid waste to whole villages along the Dnieper. Putting the torch to farms and villages. Massacring the inhabitants in ways that not even the Nazis did in their black march across the steppes. The savage Tartar hordes raping Russian females of all ages and planting inferior seed that had poisoned Russian blood forever.

And Mikhail Vishtka was hatefully conscious of his own slight build, his sloping forehead, oval-shaped face, and dark eyes that looked more like the slits of a tank turret. If there was Asian blood in him, he thought, then there was only one way to purify himself—to kill a part of himself by killing the spawn.

Without looking at the Mongols, Vishtka kept pacing, back and forth in front of the prisoners. The night seemed to weigh down upon him as he felt the strain of his duty. Behind Vishtka, three black-camoued Antonov AN-24 transport planes were grounded on the valley floor. There, SPETSNAZ commandos rolled huge crates down the aft ramps. For a moment, contemplating his next strategy, Vishtka watched those commandos break open the crates. The crates housed the parts of four Mil Mi-24 Hind helicopter gunships.

Strategy, he thought. He would make his move within moments.

The yak herd, he noticed, had been rounded up. Commandos toting AK-47s and RPK light machine guns surrounded the grunting animals. The commandos were waiting for the order.

From somewhere behind him, Vishtka heard his translator, Sergeant Sergei Jenenkov, interrogating the village khan, Timur Bhantaj. It was no mere coincidence, Vishtka decided, that the village had been named after the Mongol conqueror who was a descendant of Genghis Khan. A student of history, Vishtka knew that Tamerlane had founded the Timurid dynasty, ruling Persia and southern Russia until 1500, controlling all land from the Tigris to India during that time. But Tamerlane the Mongol had died while planning to invade China. Vishtka found that amusing. It seemed all the great Mongols died just as they had paved the way for their greatest conquests. *Da*, a black sun always set on them as their days of glory faded.

Turning, Vishtka found Jenenkov was having difficulty persuading the village khan to cooperate. Vishtka needed guides and porters to help his commandos climb Makalu. Food would be no problem. After all, it was hard to argue with a man who held a rifle on you, Vishtka thought. At the moment, commandos were scavenging through the yurts, pilfering whatever food and water they could lay their hands on. According to recon photos, the wreckage of the high-altitude reconnaissance planes, SR-71s, Moskva assumed, was scattered somewhere up Makalu I at about the 20,000-foot mark. It would be a long and difficult ascent, Vishtka knew. But both invigorating and challenging, too. Even at fifty-five years of age, Vishtka was in top physical condition. And he knew, SPETSNAZ commandos were required to pass harsh physical fitness tests that might break Olympic athletes.

Exhaling a pent-up breath, feeling the chill bite through his white windsuit, Vishtka turned his attention on the weapons confiscated from the yurts. Curved sabers and bejeweled daggers, much like the Cossack *shasqa* and *kindjal*. Tough bows made of horn and sinew and covered with some kind of waterproof lacquer. But it was the kukri fighting knives that captured Vishtka's eye. Stooping, he fisted one of the kukris, pulling a heavy leather sheathe and belt from the pile. A cruel smile tugging at the corners of bloodless lips, Vishtka ran the tip of his forefinger over twenty-two and a half inches of tempered steel. *Ordep Nepal*, the seal of acceptance, was engraved on the blade. Quickly, unzipping his parka, Vishtka fastened the belt and sheathe around his midsection. *Da,* the British Gurkha military knife, he decided, would be a nice souvenir from his Nepal mission. Provided, of course, he survived and succeeded.

AK-47 slung around his shoulder, Sergeant Jenenkov strode up to Vishtka. "Comrade Lieutenant General," he began, his breath pluming out, white, in the bitterly cold air, his body stiff, his expression grim. "The khan, Bhantaj, says we are like bothersome fleas that would crawl through his yurt, or pick at the sores of yaks. He will not cooperate. He would only wish to grind us into the soil beneath his foot. See us trampled in the dust, as he put it, see our dead flesh rot to ash and blown away by the wind. I tried to reason with him. It is obvious he does not see the folly of his words, Comrade Lieutenant General."

Vishtka nodded. That was all he needed to hear. "Very well, *tovaritsch*." *Chort Mongols! The stubborn pig dogs would rather die*, he thought. Wheeling, he barked at his commandos, "Begin!"

Without hesitation, the commandos triggered their assault rifles and light machine guns. Hemmed in by the circle of Soviet executioners, the yaks cried out in terror and agony as lead hellstorms of 7.62mm lead marched along their hides. Panicking, dozens of yaks attempted to break free of the ring of death. But SPETSNAZ killers drove the squealing animals back into each other with long, concentrated fusillades of full-auto slaughter, slugs chewing off their fur and flesh like the savage teeth of a carnivore. Bullets seemed to clip the horns off the animals' heads, then those heads exploded, showering chunks of fur, bone, and blood across the virgin snow. Within seconds, bloody, twitching carcasses piled up in a slick crimson wash. It was overkill, Vishtka decided, listening to the din of autofire rolling over him, watching as lead continued to pulp the animals into the hard-packed soil. But the lieutenant general hoped his point was made. Animals first, then their masters.

Autofire blistered the air until the commandos expended every last round in their clips. With pleasure, Vishtka listened as the killing shots echoed off the behemoth wall of rock many miles northeast of Tamerlane. Makalu I. The Leviathan.

The challenge.

Vishtka saw that the villagers were indifferent to the massacre. These Mongols are indeed a strange and stubborn people, he thought. They were unafraid of death. In that respect, he decided, the Mongol and the Russian shared something in common. Very well. A show of brutality was the only last possible resort.

"See if the khan will cooperate now," he told Jenenkov. The lieutenant general waited impatiently as Jenenkov walked up to the khan. Out of the corner of his eye, Vishtka looked at the khan as Jenenkov talked to him in the Mongol tongue. The khan was a short, muscular Mongol with shoulder-length hair as black as coal. He had a pencil-thin mustache that drooped well below his chin. Without a doubt, Bhantaj was fierce-looking, Vishtka decided, a Mongol demon who could well have ridden the Russian steppes on one of those shaggy, small Przevalsky wild horses in a previous life. *This khan is one tough old pjos.*

"He says he will disgrace the memory of the great Genghis Khan," Jenenkov called back to Vishtka, "by being the lapdog of Russian beasts."

Enough, Vishtka thought. He took several steps toward the captive Sherpas, reaching inside his parka. The 9mm Makarov seemed to leap from inside Vishtka's parka, as if it had a life of its own. In less than two blinks of an eye, the Makarov barked three times. Three deadly cracks, and 9mm slugs cored through the foreheads of an old man, a young woman, and her son. The victims toppled to the ground as if they'd been poleaxed, blood and brains smearing over the yak hair of the yurts behind the fallen corpses.

"What does the stubborn khan say now, Comrade Sergeant?" Vishtka snarled.

A leaden hush dropped over the village. More echoes of killing shots. Raw hatred stared back at Lieutenant General Vishtka of the SPETSNAZ Red Star.

Vishtka, feeling the vengeful eyes boring into him, let the Makarov lower by his side. He waited long moments for the khan to answer. Then, the khan began talking, indeed could not stop talking. A full two minutes later, Sergeant Jenenkov reported to the lieutenant general.

"It would seem the khan has come to his senses, Comrade Lieutenant General. He does not wish for us *Russian beasts* to slaughter his people. He says he will cooperate. He also told me something that might be of interest to us. Perhaps a very alarming development."

"*Da?* What?" Vishtka snapped.

"He says we are not the only ones who are interested in going up the Leviathan. He says there are foreigners here. White men. They speak English. Three days ago they arrived and hired out an expedition force of Sherpas. He gave his people permission to go with the foreigners because they were paid up front and were treated decently."

Vishtka heard the warning bells in his head. "CIA?"

Jenenkov shrugged. "It is possible, *da?*"

"Possible? Comrade Sergeant, you are to interrogate the khan further. Find out how many foreigners he saw, or heard of. Find out where they are. If they are close by, and if they saw us come in, there is a chance they might have pulled out. Perhaps to regroup. Perhaps to wait for reinforcements."

"Pull out? But to where?"

"I am not sure, Comrade Sergeant," Vishtka growled. "That is why we have people inside Kathmandu—to cover our backs. I want one full squad rounded up immediately. I want our operatives inside the capital alerted. They are to canvass the city and the surrounding countryside until they find these foreigners. When found, and I do mean *when found,* Comrade Sergeant, these foreigners are to be executed without delay. I do not need to be climbing Makalu with a pack of CIA *kalorshniks* breathing down our necks. *Ponimayo?*"

"*Da.* Understood. But surely this should come as no

74

surprise to you, Comrade Lieutenant General. The GRU did expect a team of CIA criminals to show up in Nepal."

"I am well aware of the briefing given us by the Main Intelligence Directorate, *tovaritsch*. You will tell the khan this, too. Should he not provide us with the same number of porters and guides, should he not cooperate with us fully, he and his family will die. I will shoot them dead just like that," he said, tight-lipped, nodding at the corpses, watching the blood and the gray matter leaking from their shattered skulls for a second, hoping that his stare spoke louder than any threat could. Then he rested a grim eye on the bloody carcasses. "And like that."

Pivoting to return to his interrogation of Bhantaj, Sergeant Jenenkov left Vishtka by himself. Holstering his Makarov, Lieutenant General Vishtka of the SPETSNAZ Red Star Task Force stared at the imposing Makalu massif. Indeed, he thought, his task was grim enough without CIA gangsters chasing them up and down the Leviathan. Whoever the foreigners were, they would have to be dealt with immediately. No delays. No excuses.

For he would not be able to offer Moskva any excuses if he failed.

He would simply be exiled to Siberia. Or shot dead right in the Kremlin.

Her breasts jiggled before his eyes. Sprenger felt himself unable to tear his gaze off those luscious white melons.

"As a dog returns to its vomit, so a fool repeats his folly," Sprenger said to Torquemada, finally looking away from the tall, naked blonde on the stage and sipping his beer.

"Where did that come from, friend Sprenger?"

"Proverbs. Twenty-six: eleven."

They sat in a corner booth inside the Babylon I. Sprenger, paranoid about strangers, as always, scanned the crowd, searching for hostiles. Laughing men swilling beer, he noticed. Fools pissing their money away by stuffing bills inside the garter of some whore who would take their money and go home and fuck her boyfriend tonight, he thought. Maybe it was the loud rock music grinding through his brain that was making him so edgy. Maybe it was his own dammed-up lust that he was unable to take care of right then. Maybe the beer was going straight to his head.

And maybe, just maybe, it was the warning they'd gotten from Special Operations Division back at Langley before embarking on their Everglades trackdown of Vic Gabriel. *Do not, we repeat, do not fail this time like you did in Tunisia.*

That was all they said. That was all they had to say.

The warning was clear. If Gabriel and his renegade commandos kicked their asses again . . . well, Sprenger knew both he and Torquemada would have to be looking over their shoulders for shadows. Shadows with guns.

Try as he might, Sprenger couldn't relax. Normally, he enjoyed the decadence of strip joints. The lewd, drunken behavior. Naked dancing girls hustling the patrons and making promises they had no intention of fulfilling. Sprenger would have guessed that after the massacre at the Babylon III the other night, all of Manny Vitelli's strip joints would have shut down. At least for a day or so out of respect for the late mobster. Hell, it was business as usual at all the Babylons except III. And the Babylon III was only shut down for repairs—and to mop the blood and guts up off the floor. More than likely, Sprenger knew, someone had gladly stepped in and filled old Manny's shoes without shedding one tear for the dead boss. *Fuck 'em and feed 'em to the worms,* Sprenger thought, then felt the ice shiver down his spine. Maybe Langley was saying the same thing about him at the moment.

"You know what I meant."

Torquemada's voice jarred Sprenger from his dark thoughts. "Huh. Oh, yes. I was just thinking out loud, that's all. Maybe we're all fools who never learn from our mistakes. We seem to return to whatever it is that can be our undoing. We seek that which is bad for us. We chase our vices and give glory to them."

"You're troubled?"

"Aren't you?"

"Should I be?"

Sprenger scowled. Suddenly, he found himself hating his comrade in cloak-and-dagger and assassination. Torquemada was a little too damn smug for his liking.

"You know what will happen if we don't get those Sphinx black boxes back," Sprenger reminded Torquemada.

"Stop worrying. We've got the best men on it. And I'm not talking about Gabriel and his cutthroat mercenaries."

"I just wish we were there in Nepal."

"We don't need to be. Our man here in Miami is keeping us updated by the hour."

Which brought Sprenger to another problem. "Now that the Russians have arrived on the scene, we could be looking at a bloodbath."

"So? If the Russians take care of Gabriel and his hellhounds, that's just four less targets for us to terminate when this thing's over."

"Right," Sprenger said, but he didn't agree. "What about Saunders?"

"What about him?" Torquemada asked, and sipped at his beer.

"The Company wants him terminated, too. Because of his personal vendetta against Saunders, Gabriel could still be of use to us in helping to track him down."

"Somehow, somewhere, someday, friend Sprenger," Torquemada assured, "Michael Saunders will turn up. Don't worry."

Don't worry, Sprenger thought. Sure, why worry?

Hell, it was only their lives they were talking about anyway.

As he fixed his gaze on the naked blonde ahead, Sprenger was thinking about worms. And ashes and dust. And Death.

His own.

Chapter 7

Captain Thomas Blackwell was dying, and he knew there was nothing, short of a miracle, that could save him. According to his Rolex, it was now five days and thirteen hours since he'd ejected from the cockpit of his SR-71. Parachuting to earth, in the slipstream of his flamed-out reconnaissance plane, *Lightning Bolt*, seemed like an eternity ago. Clinging to the spines of icy ridges for all he was worth. Eventually mustering the courage to slide down on his haunches to whatever looked like a platform below. Should he hit a slick sheet of ice on any of those jagged, terraced platforms, he would sail off into oblivion, plunge for the mist, thousands of feet below. Perhaps, he had thought in moments of despair, when feeling his utter isolation at the top of the world and gazing up at a sky that seemed to sit right on the summit, plummeting from the face of the Leviathan would end his misery. And his troubles. But no. He was a survivor, and he believed in himself. A fighter, yes, he would make it off that mountain. He would see civilization again. He would embrace his wife and children. He would feel the warmth and the comfort and the safety of his own home in the suburbs of Denver.

And he had the Sphinx black box tucked under his arm. Somehow, he was determined to salvage success from disaster. If he made it back home, he would be something of a national hero, he thought. *What a stupid thought*, he chided himself. *I'm on my last leg, and I've got visions of camera bulbs flashing in my head. Christ, you idiot, you.*

Was he losing his mind? he wondered.

He was scared, that much he knew.

His body reminded him that Death was calling. Indeed, he began to think, Death was laughing at him in the winds that screamed and swirled around him, hurling spindrifts of snow against his unprotected face. A face that was no longer raw and aching, but cracked and frozen. A face that was now numb, like his hands and feet. He had to keep moving. Had to. If he stopped, the pain would go away. A warmth would settle over him and grip him in a cementlike vise. Then he would feel sleepy.

In sleep, would come Death.

His empty belly had long since stopped grumbling in protest for want of food. He had drained the last of the water from his canteen two days ago and resorted to eating snow. Damn those idiots in the think tanks back at the Pentagon, he thought. They were safe and warm, and yeah, smug somewhere, riding around Wondertown, D.C., in their fancy cars and wondering about their errant spy fly-boys. Little did those brilliant engineers of the modified spy plane know that the added weight of the Sidewinders had done something, he was sure, to cause his SR-71, *Lightning Bolt,* to later flame out at a critical time. Worse, as if they'd had a mind of their own, the missiles had launched from the wings of *Lightning Bolt* as he'd been swooping toward the Russian base near the Chinese border. Accident? Oversight? Or sabotage? Whatever, his attempt to get a better look at that Russian base from fifty thousand feet had started the whole disaster, one that could well blow up into an international nightmare. Gary Powers would just become a small paragraph in some history book. Hell, should this dark incident come to light, he thought, his name and his mission would fill up whole books and knock everything else off the best-seller list. Then sorrow tightened a lump in his throat. At least he hadn't been blown out of the sky like his friend and fellow spy pilot, Captain Jim Brighton. Jim was dead, and his troubles were over.

Shivering in his thermal-insulated windsuit, Blackwell briefly recalled his ejection and descent from *Lightning Bolt*. The whole damn fall came flashing back to him suddenly, eerie in some way he couldn't quite understand. He had fallen, using the risers in a desperate attempt to veer himself away from the mountains. But he had been sucked into a vortex of gale-force winds that drove him toward the face of the behemoth. Trembling against the bitter lash of icy wind, he remembered his head-on descent toward the flaming wreckage of *Lightning Bolt*. Like a magnet, Makalu had drawn him toward its face. An icy face that had seemed to grin back at him under a blinding blaze of sunlight.

Eerie, yeah.

Miracles, no way.

He was on his own, a living dead man with nothing but a hope and a prayer. With nothing but the brutal elements that wanted to eat him alive. With nothing but a wall of ice and rock that wanted to hurl him from off the top of the world.

Blackwell looked up, squinting against the harsh glare, the sunlight washing over the snow-blanketed face of the Makalu massif like a beacon.

A beacon from hell, he grimly thought. Without protective goggles, it even hurt to keep his eyes open.

Three hours ago dawn had broken over the Himalayas in a glazing flood of light. High above Blackwell, giant billowy clouds wreathed the summit of Makalu. Everest and Lhotse were some ten miles northwest, he believed, but he couldn't see the granite behemoths because of the clouds and the sawtooth ridgeline that jutted in a humpback away from the face of the Leviathan, a thousand feet or more above. According to his map, the Barun Glacier was east. And the Arun Gorge was below, far, far below the cloud bank that hugged the face of Makalu. He wasn't sure how high up he was, but he guessed he was easily stuck on the Leviathan at around the 20,000-foot mark. Thank God, he thought, the weather would hold, and the skies wouldn't open up and drench him in snow. The slopes and ridges were already caked with two to three feet of snow now. And far, far below, Captain Blackwell could hear the ominous rumbles. If he kept spining the razorback ridge, he could stay above the avalanches. He had no desire to be buried alive beneath acres of snow sloughing off the slopes under the burning curtain of intense sunlight. Then again, he realized he couldn't keep moving horizontally. Eventually, the ridge would peter out.

He would have to go down. He would have to find a crevasse and pray for the best. The only use his Beretta 92F, the official sidearm of the U.S. military, and his favored British Sykes-Fairbairn commando dagger could be put to was if he encountered a snow leopard and had to slay the beast for food. Or came face-to-face with the yeti, he grimly joked to himself, and had to kill the big bastard for a fur coat. Without rope, pitons, and crampons, among other climbing essentials, he knew it would be impossible to descend if he came to a sheer vertical face. But he had to try. Something. Anything. At least, he bitterly thought, he had a pack of smokes and a Zippo with a new flint and fresh Ronson lighter fluid. He could always smoke a cigarette in his last moments and curse the mountain gods before he laid down in the snow and went to sleep forever.

Laughing out loud at the insanity of his predicament, Blackwell looked down the spine of the ridge. Then he saw it and felt his heart skip a beat.

The hand jutted out of the snow. Blackwell experienced a fresh stab of terror as he sidled down the ridge on his haunches. He couldn't believe his eyes as his gaze fixed on the ice-crusted fingers, curled like the talons of some predatory bird.

The wind soughed.

Blackwell shivered, frozen by some feeling of primeval dread and violence he couldn't understand. Suddenly, he was alone. With the dead.

With a grim reminder of his own fate.

Quickly, almost frantically, he brushed the snow off the arm. It took a full three minutes before he uncovered the corpse. Icicles hung from the man's beard, and ice had frozen over his goggles, the face a blistered mask mottled by snow that seemed ingrained in the flesh.

Bile burned into Blackwell's throat. There was an ice pick in the corpse's hand. Blackwell tried to wrench the ice pick out of the dead man's hand, but it was frozen solid in that hand, as if the tool were an extension of the unfeeling flesh. With his dagger, feeling relief and horror at the same time, Blackwell hacked the dead man's fingers off. As he tugged at the ice pick, strips of flesh began to peel off the dead man's palm and fingers like the rind of an orange.

Blackwell retched.

Wiping the saliva off his mouth, Blackwell finished the grim chore of prying the ice pick free. Then he saw the top of the rucksack. There was rope fastened around the corpse's midsection.

Oh, my God, Blackwell thought.

Yanking on the rope, Blackwell felt the leaden weight . . . on the other end.

More dead men.

Climbers who had gone in search of . . . of what? he wondered. Glory? To top the summit because it was there? *Christ*, he thought, *I'm here and if I get off this godforsaken rock, I've got no desire at all ever to come back*.

Who the dead were, and exactly how they had died, Blackwell didn't know, wasn't sure if he even cared at the moment. Now, if there was food in those rucksacks. . . .

Twenty minutes later, Captain Blackwell had dug four bodies out of the snow with his gloved hands. Having chipped away at ice and snow with vicious strokes, Blackwell knew he had exhausted his final reserves of energy. Food was his only thought. Nourishment. Strength. Energy.

Hope.

Captain Thomas Blackwell dug through the rucksacks. He found ten ice screws and four braking devices.

But no food.

Fuck it. He couldn't eat ice screws.

Despair gnawing into his guts, Captain Blackwell slumped back against the spine of the ridge. He wanted to weep, but he didn't even have the strength to push the tears into the corners of his eyes. Just barely, he found the energy to curse.

The wind laughed at him.

The snow danced along the ridge.

The clouds weighed down on Captain Blackwell with a crushing force that seemed alive in the icy air.

Without food, he knew he would die. He had maybe another day, at the most. It didn't really seem to matter to him that he had the necessary equipment at least to attempt a descent down the mountain. Hell, he knew the ridge had to lead to a glacier. And the glacier to a valley. But descent would take days and days. Maybe weeks. Maybe longer, if the weather turned savage.

Without food . . .

From the pocket of his windsuit he fished out his pack of Camel unfiltereds. He pulled out a cigarette, placed the butt on his cracked lips. With his trusty Zippo, he torched the smoke.

Then a thought formed in his head as he looked at the ice-crusted faces beneath him. Those unseeing eyes stared up at him. And he felt accused already. Of a crime he didn't really want to commit.

But had to in order to survive.

Captain Blackwell slid down the slope toward the dead.

Knife in hand, he asked God in heaven to forgive him for what he was about to do.

Kathmandu.

A city, both sacred and profane, resting at the edge of time. Capital of a sequestered kingdom of Sherpa mountaineers and knife-wielding Gurkha warriors, Kathmandu appeared to Vic Gabriel to be the least modernized city he'd seen in Asia.

As Attila steered the armored jeep with grim skill and steely patience through a teeming mass of humanity and sacred cows that waddled along the streets, Vic Gabriel couldn't help but feel transported back in time. Descendants of the Mongols, Newars in brightly colored garb jammed the narrow streets, staring at the jeep as if it were some alien spacecraft. The cold air stank of cow dung, sweat, and incense. Pagoda-roofed Hindu shrines rose above the wood-balconied Newar homes. Statues of Buddhist deities stood out like gargoyles in the temple shelters that the jeep passed. Yeah, the city was packed, crackling with energy, much the same way Gabriel remembered Saigon before the Fall. No soldiers here, but there were Gurkha policemen in crisp khaki pants. Then there was the underbelly, the darker side of life in Kathmandu. Without much searching, Gabriel picked out the junkies of European origin hanging around on the street corners, their bloodshot eyes hungrily seeking out the Man with their next hit. No Montagnards here, Gabriel mused, but there were Tibetan refugees mulling in the marketplace, shivering in red and black rags that hung from sparse frames. No matter where he went, Vic Gabriel always saw, and felt, the eternal struggle of mankind. The living, the dead, and the dying. The rich and the poor. And the street hustlers looking to peck their way up the order any way they could, even if it was at the expense of someone else's life and peace of mind. The more something changes . . . right . . . Man would always stand frozen in time, Gabriel thought, because he was a slave to the world. His world. His desires.

A gray sky hung over Kathmandu like a lead curtain. Somehow, the cold air and the overcast sky suited his somber mood, Gabriel thought.

With a flick of his trusty Zippo, Gabriel fired up a Marlboro. Behind him, Simms, Boolewarke, and Dillinger sat crammed together, huddled around the belted .50-caliber machine gun. There was just enough room in the jeep for their weapons. Beneath their black Army-style field jackets, each commando of Eagle Force toted his holstered sidearm.

Since hitting the LZ in the Kathmandu valley, the five of them had ridden into the city in silence. Grim silence.

The Russians were in Nepal, after all. And maybe that was all anybody needed to know.

Still, Gabriel felt it was time to break the silence and get some answers from Attila.

"Couple of questions, Attila."

Attila grunted. "Can't promise I can answer them."

"Give it a shot, huh," Gabriel said, a hard edge to his voice. "Why, exactly, do we need to come here?"

"I told you. My contact's here. I need a full rundown on the Russian situation—numbers, armament. Anything else?" Attila asked, then braked the jeep at the end of a long, narrow street, near the massive entrance of a shrine. Over the entrance to the shrine was a statue of the Hindu goddess Kali. There, worshipers climbed wooden ladders to attach offerings of greenery to the goddess.

"Not at the moment," Gabriel said after a moment's pause. "I'll let you know if something else comes to mind."

Attila hopped out of the jeep. "You do that, soldier."

"Dutch," Gabriel said, opening his door, blowing smoke, "you stay here with the stash."

"What happens if some Gurkha copper gets nosy?"

Boolewarke asked a legitimate question. Standing outside the jeep, Gabriel looked to Attila for an answer.

"Don't fret," the Company op growled, his voice nearly drowned out by the yelling of street vendors, the laughter of children, and the buzz of motorbikes that seemed to be the main source of transportation in Kathmandu. "It's covered. Do you hotshot mercs think the CIA came here unprepared?"

"Not at all," Johnny Simms remarked, filing out of the jeep behind Zac Dillinger.

Attila squared his shoulders, his hand draped over the butt of his .45 Colt automatic. "What's that supposed to mean?"

"Nothin'. Let's get the show on the road, cowboy," Simms said. "It's gettin' cold out here."

Attila grunted, then told Gabriel, "Follow me. And keep your smart mouths shut."

"Whatever you say, Hun honey," Dillinger cracked.

Attila scowled at the ex-P.I., a dangerous glint in the operative's cold eyes. Finally, the moment passed, and Attila faced front and walked off.

Moments later, the three commandos rounded a corner behind Attila. Ragged urchins, running wild in the streets, bumped into Gabriel. A cab sped past the men and ox dung suddenly spattered the stone wall, less than inches from Attila's face. Attila muttered a curse over his shoulder at the cabbie.

A wry grin cracked Dillinger's lips. "A sign of things to come, Hun?"

"What did I tell you about your mouth, wiseass?"

Attila rasped out of the corner of his face. Halfway down the narrow alley, Attila stopped in front of a heavy steel door. "You go in here runnin' your mouths, you'll never see these streets again. Personally, I don't give a damn if you live or die. But I don't need to get carved up by some Mongol's knife because I can't keep you hotshot dogs of war on a leash. Got me?"

"Where are you taking us?" Gabriel wanted to know.

Attila showed the commandos a cruel smile. "Down under. Into hell, friend. A side of this city that not many people know about. Or want to know about."

Attila rapped on the door. A second later the door squeaked open on rusty hinges.

A burly Mongol with a bald dome and a Fu Manchu mustache, donning leather and fur, stared at Attila, then raked a hard eye over the three commandos.

"Atlas is expecting us," Attila told the doorman.

The Mongol grunted, stepped aside. His hand was wrapped around the golden hilt of a long, curved saber.

He could smell an Ivan from a mile away, Henry van Boolewarke thought. All the potato faces smelled like vodka, but stank like the shit of the steppes. Christ's eyes, he hated those red bastards!

At the end of the street, Boolewarke easily spotted the ten men in black leather trench coats. With long strides, spread out in a phalanx, they shoved their way through the Newar crowds, nearly bowling down several men on motorbikes in their haste to move down the street. Those goons were moving with purpose, Boolewarke thought. *And they're not your everyday normal Newar aluminum salesmen either or some chum out to sell you a bronze statue of Buddha*. Several of those men held their hands against the sides of their trench coats. As if they were trying to balance weapons too big for holsters, the Dutchman decided. Submachine pistols.

Moments later, three beaten-up Peugeots pulled into the mouth at the end of the street. Intently, Boolewarke watched as another ten men piled out of those cars. Those men wore black camous and moved with the grim purpose of killers on the hunt, too. Boolewarke saw the point man in the first hit team wave toward the second group. He thought he heard, *"Bysstryj! Davay!"* Which meant "faster," or "move it," in Russian. Russian voices, though—the Dutchman definitely heard the Ivanspeak.

Goons, *ja*, Boolewarke thought, watching as the first squad linked up with the second team of hitters, their eyes roving the crowds. Then, spreading out in a ragged line, they rounded the corner. The same direction Vic Gabriel and the others had gone!

The Ivans were there for a hit.

That was all Henry van Boolewarke needed to know. To hell with watching the weapons stash. When he'd heard the four of them might be locking horns with Ivan on this outing, Boolewarke recalled the surge of energy he'd felt back in the USA. Who else but Ivan would gain by fomenting the unrest in South Africa, Boolewarke's homeland? No, Boolewarke might not agree with the RSA's apartheid policies, but South Africa was still his home, and the Afrikaners were still his blood. No doubt about it, Ivan wanted the richest country in all of Africa under the hammer and sickle, Boolewarke knew. If he didn't fight Ivan wherever and whenever he found him . . . well, how could any man forsake three hundred years of roots and still be proud of himself and his heritage? If nothing else, then Boolewarke knew Ivan was standing by in the countries surrounding the RSA, sharpening his blade and ready to make his move once anarchy and a bloodbath of a revolution swept through South Africa. Oh, the horror was coming, Boolewarke believed. His homeland was sitting on a human time bomb. And the damn Ivans were feeding the cancer with arms and money every day. Training and supplying the terrorists and guerrillas. If it hadn't been for Moscow's influence over black guerrillas, Boolewarke knew his ranch might still be standing in the Transvaal.

The horror had already been visited upon Henry van Boolewarke. Memories the Dutchman would take with him into the grave. But not before Ivan paid a price for his rape of Africa.

Grim-faced, Boolewarke fisted the M60 machine gun. Thrusting the door open, he stepped out into the street, unmindful of the noise around him and the high-pitched voices of Buddhists chanting in prayer from the nearby shrine. Letting the belt of push-through 7.62mm NATO links drape in front of him, he thumbed the safety off, jacked back the cocking-lever handle.

Henry van Boolewarke didn't give a damn if all eyes were watching him or not as he strode away from the jeep.

The Dutchman had come to Nepal for one thing, and one thing only.

To kill some Ivans.

Behind the big Afrikaner with the belted M60, Newars chanted in prayer to Buddha.

Chapter 8

The hashish smoke was so thick, Vic Gabriel thought
he was going to gag. If someone had walked up to him and
said, Welcome to hell, he would have replied, Yeah, I'm
there, all right.

And he was.

At least two dozen large, round wooden tables jammed
the opium den. Candles on the tables, or a dozen naked
lightbulbs, hung from the ceiling, lit the den, washing a
ghostly orange hue over the crowd. There was one main
room, packed with Mongols, Gurkhas, Newars, turbaned
Arabs, Europeans, and men of other nationalities and
races that Gabriel couldn't determine, men shadowed by
the smoke clouds and murky light. It was wall-to-wall
sweltering humanity, a mob indulging in just about every
vice under the sun. Rupees and tugriks, the Mongolian
monetary unit, flew across the tables where fur-and-leather-
garbed men rolled dice made of buffalo horn or elephant
tusk. Everyone in that main room was either sucking the
Nepali liquor, *rakshi*, from huge golden gourds that would
have made the German stein microscopic in comparison,
or puffing on ornately carved wooden pipes with bowls
stuffed with hash or opium. Combat senses on full alert for
some treachery Attila wasn't going to warn him about,
Gabriel eyed the armament in that den. Huge curved
sabers and Gurkha fighting knives. Hip- or shoulder-
holstered Turkish 9mm Kirikkale pistols and Russian 7.62mm

Tokarevs. Mini-Uzis, and submachine pistols that Gabriel couldn't even begin to identify.

Beaded curtains hung from the archways of three offshoots to the main room. As Gabriel spotted the painted women in garish dresses of questionable Asian taste, he figured there was more going on in the opium den than just drinking and smoking and gambling. A lot more.

"How would you like to take a little R and R here, VG?" Zac Dillinger said as the three commandos followed Attila, the operative weaving his way through the crowd, the four of them drawing suspicious looks from faces in the throng. "Hedonism, hedonism, and more hedonism. Christ, I could piss away a year's pay here!"

The hell of it was, Gabriel almost thought Bad Zac was serious.

The sounds of raucous laughter and shouting assaulting his ears, Gabriel said, "Not on my time, you wouldn't, so get your head right."

"All right, all right, I wasn't serious anyway. These Asian whores," Dillinger said, as a woman with more money tied up in the diamonds and gold on her ears and around her neck than most Third World countries earned from their gross national product last year slid up to the ex-P.I., "would probably cut your balls off and sell 'em for yak soup."

The whore laid her hands on Dillinger's shoulders. "Big strong American man looking for luckie-luckie?"

Dillinger shrugged her hands off his shoulders. "That's fuckie-fuckie in American. And it looks like your luckie-luckie just ran out, babe. We're on a mission from God—Uncle Sam."

"Uncle Sam want fuckie-fuckie?" the whore called after Dillinger.

Johnny Simms chuckled, but there was no mirth in the sound, Gabriel noticed. They were all worried, and they had every right to be looking over their shoulders.

Gabriel couldn't shake the feeling that trouble was about to rear its ugly hydra's head. Since his days with the Special Forces in Vietnam, Gabriel had seen and dealt out death. Plenty of death. Too much death. He had become so familiar with death during the violence of his life that he'd developed a sixth sense, one that would warn him when the Man with the scythe was lurking nearby.

Finally, Attila led the three commandos to a table in the far corner of the room. The one man seated at that table was a big, beefy guy with a salt-and-pepper mustache and black hair with touches of gray around the temples. He sat with his back to the stone wall, candlelight flickering over his grizzled face. Attila's contact, Atlas, Gabriel figured. Another cold, heartless CIA gun-for-hire. Just more trouble, as far as Gabriel was concerned.

Attila pulled up a chair and sat down. As Attila's contact gave the three commandos a hard eyeballing, Gabriel, Dillinger, and Simms also sat.

"This them?" Atlas grunted.

"Yeah," Attila replied. "The ex-Recces hero is out in the jeep."

"They packing?"

"Cannons."

"Figures."

Gabriel wasn't sure what that was supposed to mean, but he didn't press it.

"What's the situation?" Gabriel asked.

"Hey, soldier," Attila growled, "I ask the questions here, all right?"

"So start asking," Gabriel shot back. "We've got a rock to climb, remember?"

"And if we sit here much longer, breathin' in the fumes," Johnny Simms put in, sniffing at the air as cumulus clouds of hash smoke drifted over the black ex-merc, "we may get high enough to fly up those slopes. Know what I mean?"

"I asked for some tough soldiers and they send us comedians," Atlas growled at Attila.

"They got a track record," Attila said, and shrugged. "Who knows? They might cut it."

"Yeah, well, cut this," Atlas began. "Mother Russia landed her finest in Tamerlane about fifteen hours ago. A SPETSNAZ Mountain-Airborne Task Force, so the wonder boys back home tell me. And they got that straight from their mole inside Moscow, so I've got no reason to doubt who they are that we'll be facing. Some tough, tough sons of bitches, you can bank on it." Atlas talked only to Attila, as if Gabriel and his commandos weren't even at the table. "We're looking at maybe four, five squads of Ivans. Three Antonovs grounded in a yak pasture and a ZSU-23-4 Quad self-propelled cannon pointed skyward like they're expecting a fleet of F-15s. They already shot up half the village and slaughtered a whole herd of yaks, so I gotta believe they're serious about getting back those Sphinx black boxes, too."

"What was the point to the killing?" Gabriel asked.

"Who knows how Ivan thinks, soldier?" Atlas answered. "Ask the *mujahadeen* in Afghanistan why the Russians booby-trapped kids' toys that blow up in their faces and spray the countryside with chemicals that'll turn you into a pile of yellow-and-green crap before you even have a chance to hit the ground. From what our expedition's *sirdar* says, it looks like Ivan needed some of those Sherpas to lug food and gear up Makalu, so they corralled about twenty-five of the villagers. And the killing? Hell, maybe SPETSNAZ just wanted to make the point that the Sherpa porters shouldn't expect to get paid."

"Except in blood," Dillinger commented, cryptic, his expression cold.

"Question," Gabriel said.

"What did I just tell you?" Attila rasped.

Gabriel injected ice into his eyes. "Shut up."

Attila started to stand, fury storming into his eyes. Then Atlas placed a restraining hand on Attila's shoulder.

"Forget it, it's all right," Atlas said. "We're all in this together, so let 'em ask away. We got enough to worry about without flexing muscle with each other."

Attila sat. "All right, talk."

"What about this Expedition Force Leviathan?" Gabriel asked.

Atlas fired up a Camel deathstick with a flick of his Zippo. "What about it, soldier?"

"How many CIA guns have you got, other than you two?"

"Listen, soldier," Atlas said, leaning up, "I know all about your problems with the Company. I know about your father and that screw-up in Paris. I know about Mike Saunders, and if you think the Company's setting you and your special renegade hit team up for the wrong edge of the blade, think again. They want your skills, because you're qualified to kill."

"They want expendables," Gabriel said.

"What do you think we are?" Attila said. "Future candidates for the Oval Office?"

"As for the killing part," Atlas said, and blew smoke at the commandos, "when I see some done by you wiseguys, I may become a believer."

"Does your *sirdar* and his Sherpas know what they're getting into?" Dillinger asked.

"They do now," Atlas replied. "And they're loaded with all the weapons of their ancestral khans, crap the Smithsonian would pay top dollar for in a fartbeat."

Gabriel fired up a Marlboro. "Well, let me tell you, if they're in this now for vengeance, we'd be better going it alone."

"I agree. We don't need a bunch of kill-crazy Mongols on the warpath," Dillinger said. "They start letting the arrows fly at the wrong time—"

"Listen, soldier," Atlas cut in, "they're going, and that's final and I don't wanna hear a bunch of crap about it. And who asked you anyway? To tell you the truth, I don't particularly need to be lugging a hundred or more pounds of gear and food through the valleys and up the slopes of Makalu on top of my weapons. As for arrows flying, the *sirdar* has assured me he and his people won't go off half-cocked when we catch up to Ivan."

"Which means that by now the Russians have got about a half day or more head start on us," Gabriel said. "We ought to be rolling east instead of sitting here jaw-fucking. Time's killing us."

"Hold your horses, soldiers," Atlas said, his gray eyes narrowing behind a drifting veil of smoke. "Ivan came more prepared than we'd thought."

"How's that?" Gabriel wanted to know.

"Helicopter-gunship prepared, that's how. Mi-24 Hinds, to be exact."

Dillinger whistled.

"Yeah, keep whistling, clown," Atlas growled. "Those warbirds have enough firepower on 'em to blow us all off the face of Makalu before we hit the first mantelshelf."

"I take it then you've got all the necessary gear and we're ready to roll?"

"It's not that simple," Atlas informed Gabriel.

When Atlas hesitated, puffing nervously on his cigarette, Gabriel felt an ominous rumbling stir in his guts. "What isn't so simple?"

"The winter snows came early this year," Atlas answered. "There's no telling how much snow the mountain gods dumped on us. It's going to make the hike a whole helluva lot tougher, that much I can tell ya. So, if we don't get buried beneath an avalanche, we've got Ivan hit teams to worry about. Now... we'll be going up the southern side of Makalu, lots of valleys and glaciers, crevasses, and some hard vertical climbing. That's straight from the *sirdar's* mouth. Unless, of course, Captain Blackwell landed a lot farther down the mountain than we figured, I'm hoping we won't have to climb over twenty thousand feet. My guess is that, if the weather holds, the Russians intend to use those warbirds for recon and recovery. Meaning, if they spot Blackwell, they'll snatch him off the mountain."

"So, why didn't the CIA just bring in their own armada of warbirds and do the same?" Simms asked.

Atlas's lips slitted into a sneer. "If we'd wanted a dogfight over the Himalayas, soldier, yeah, we could've packed up a whole fleet of AH-64 Apaches with Hellfire missiles and gone toe-to-toe with Ivan. Media exposure, though, is the last thing anybody wants in this. We're to go about this real quiet. Up and down, in and out. Any problems, you come to me or Attila. Any questions, likewise. Now, if there aren't any more questions, I'll get back to my jeep. We've got a tough drive ahead of us, at least ten to twelve hours. It'll be slow going. But aerial recon managed to pick out the easiest way to Tamerlane. We'll swing south to bypass the high country, then . . ."

The look in Atlas's eyes, as the operative stared right past Gabriel, warned the ex–Special Forces warrior that something was wrong.

Deadly wrong.

Snapping his head sideways, Gabriel found out that he'd been dead right about trouble following them into the opium den.

And Death had just stepped into hell.

Simms and Dillinger spotted the men in trench coats, too. They were filing through the doorway, grim eyes searching the crowd, hands already digging inside those trench coats. Thinly veiled behind the hash smoke, they moved, swift dark silhouettes in the gloomy light.

Through the wafting gray sheets of smoke, Vic Gabriel made eye contact with one of the trench-coated strangers.

Somehow they looked familiar to Gabriel, or perhaps he should've recognized them. Or. . .

"Russians!" Atlas warned.

That was all Vic Gabriel and his commandos needed to hear.

The Russian hitters dug out weapons. A split second later, Gabriel saw the assassins tracking his way with Tokarevs and Czech M61 submachine pistols.

The three commandos of Eagle Force clawed beneath their field jackets for leather.

Shrill female screams ripped through the opium den as a lead beeline of slugs stitched Mongols on a deadly tracking path toward the Americans.

Chapter 9

The potential killing field stared up at Henry van Boolewarke from below.

From the gaping mouth of hell, he thought. And hell was exactly where the Dutchman intended to send the pack of Marxist assassins. The Dutchman was going to grab *potential* by its jagged tail of deadly lightning. Hurl bolts of death down at the Russian killers he loved to hate so much. *Goddamn their black-hearted souls to hell anyway for their murdering, lying ways!*

And the Dutchman was going to ride the thunder out. One way or another.

Blazing into the eye of the storm.

He was in this one for the long haul, and he intended to see Ivan bite down on his own flesh, drink his own blood. *The only way to get rid of garbage forever is to burn it.*

Moving down the three flights of stone steps, all but three killers in the Russian hit teams had surged through the doorway, their weapons already chattering and chewing up flesh. For a second, Boolewarke smelled the pungent stench of hash smoke and wondered just why in the hell the CIA would bring them here into an abyss of thieves, killers, and addicts in the first place. Bring or lead? Right. The mission was making less sense to Boolewarke by the minute. Somebody, he was sure, was setting the four of them up to take a fall. A hard fall.

Then the Dutchman fixed grim deathsights on his targets.

Stepping over the outstretched body of the doorman a Russian killer had shot in the face at point-blank range, Boolewarke let the M60 machine gun rip. In the close confines of the narrow corridor, the M60 pealed like rolling thunder, big 7.62mm NATO slugs ripping into the backs of the Ivans at the bottom of the steps, hot shell casings twirling around Boolewarke's face of rage and vengeance as he rode the recoil of the big maneater.

Screaming, the three Russians danced a jig of death, thrashing in the roaring M60 blaze as 7.62mm NATO lead marched up their legs and backs, gouging open big holes in their chests and exploding their heads like rotten melons. Dead before they even hit the edge of the steps, they were convulsing, fingers squeezing off a burst of 7.65mm rounds from stuttering Czech M61 submachine pistols.

Swiftly, hearing the shrill cries of pain and terror, knowing he had to get into that den and spew death if Vic and the others were going to get out alive, Henry van Boolewarke bounded down the steps. He leapt over the twitching Russian corpses, burst into the den. Directly ahead, the Dutchman saw the Russian hitters mowing down the patrons in that viper's den, murderously intent on paving a bloody path for Vic Gabriel and other others. Anybody in the eye of Russian fire, Boolewarke saw, was fair game.

And it was open season on Ivan, as far as Henry van Boolewarke was concerned. *The Devil be damned in his own blood and shit!*

The Dutchman stepped into the opium den. Primed for overkill, Boolewarke turned up the heat in that place, the M60 bucking and blazing in his big fists.

Like a well-oiled machine, Gabriel, Simms, and Dillinger rolled into action. Hitting combat crouches, the three commandos triggered .44 rounds from thundering Ruger Redhawk Magnums, and three Russian killers spun as the slugs drilled into their chests, flinging them like torn scarecrows over tables. Behind Gabriel, Atlas, .45 Colt automatic springing from his holster, hurled the table up into the air.

Attila's own .45 Colt was flaming and bucking out lead, the operative driving two Russian targets into each other. Blood sprayed over the walls, lead whined off the floor, and bodies pitched through beaded curtains.

Like berserkers streaming off some Viking vessel, the Russians were tearing their way through the throng, their chattering Stechkins sweeping the mob and killing anything that moved. Mongols and Gurkhas were toppling like bowling pins under the relentless stammering barrage of Czech and Soviet Stechkin submachine pistols and the barking of Tokarev pistols. Turbaned heads were blasted apart by ComBloc lead. Screaming and cursing lanced the smoke-choked air in a half dozen languages, but the only tongue acknowledged in that free-fire zone was Death.

Realizing they were caught in a crossfire hurricane of sizzling lead, the patrons in the opium den jumped into the foray, each man seeking only to save his own skin. Swords and knives were unsheathed, mini-Uzis and submachine pistols snaking from holsters. Wild-eyed men vaulted over tables. Metal flashed and automatic weapons roared. A Russian assassin had his head cleaved off at the shoulders by the cutting edge of a Mongol blade. Another Russian killer slipped in the juices of his fallen comrade, as blood geysered from the stump of the headless SPETSNAZ assassin. For a heartbeat, the Stechkin machine pistol flamed, then the decapitated corpse, jerking around like a puppet on a string, toppled, draping itself over a whore crawling for cover beneath a table. She died a millisecond later when a SPETSNAZ commando raked her with autofire, the killer's expression damn near one of glee.

Murderous chaos descended around Gabriel as he was driven to the stone floor under the crashing weight of the table. It was every man for himself, he instantly realized, belching air, tasting stone, and cursing whoever had thrown the table down on him to cover his own ass from the flying lead. And Vic Gabriel saw the Mongol saber craning for his face.

Pinned beneath the table, the boom of hand cannons and the blister of autofire in his ears, Gabriel squeezed the Ruger Redhawk's trigger. The twisted Mongol face in Gabriel's sight melted into a death mask, the .44 slug tunneling through the Asian's fur and gouging open a bloody hole in his stomach. Blood and guts spattered the stone around Gabriel's face, and bone chips and more tattered cloth erupted from the Mongol's back. As if he'd been impaled by an invisible spear, that Mongol doubled over, catapulted by the sudden impact of Magnum lead and hurtled into a whore. With a mighty heave, the ex-CIA assassin shoved the table off him.

Johnny Simms hit the floor, rolling. Less than an eyeblink later, the Mongol blade clanged off stone where Simms's head had been. Pivoting, Dillinger crucified that Mongol to the wall with two chest-shots, fur and blood smearing Atlas's face. Wheeling, the ex-P.I. searched for Russian hitters, his twin .45 Blood and Guts specials fanning the smoke and gloom.

Through the smoke, Gabriel made out the tall, broad figure of Henry van Boolewarke on the other side of the charnel house. Surging through the doorway, the Dutchman hosed three Russians with a hot stream of 7.62mm lead, the big M60 pedaling thunder and raining death through the den. The odds were being shaved in an all-out fury.

The killing blasts cannoned, on and on, reverberating in Gabriel's ears.

On trumpet blasts from the River Styx, Gabriel thought. Kneeling, Gabriel stroked the stainless steel hand cannon's trigger again. Downrange, he saw the slug punch through an Ivan's face, the incredible muzzle velocity demolishing that face as if a wrecking ball had just dropped from the ceiling and caught that guy in his tracks, lifting him off his feet and hurling him back as if he were nothing more than a sack of potatoes. How exactly they would get out of there, Vic Gabriel didn't have the faintest idea. At the moment, his full and grim attention was focused on the enemy.

And the enemy came at them from everywhere. Survival in that hell simply meant triggering the fastest and most deadly accurate gun. Savagery and tenacity. Kick ass, take no names, and definitely don't take any prisoners, Gabriel knew.

Slugs ricocheting off the stone wall behind him, Gabriel pumped two more slugs into Mongols charging him. Flipped out on hash and opium, those Mongols raced into Death without flinching. As .44 Magnum slugs tore through their chests, pulverizing their hearts and exploding out their backs from a fist-sized wound canal, Mongol blades whirled through the air. *They just experienced the final high*, Gabriel thought, and tracked on.

Atlas bowled a Gurkha policeman to the floor as the operative bolted away from the wall. Out of the corner of his eye, Gabriel saw the Gurkha fighting knife whirling through the air, a blur that seemed to part the smoke as it streaked toward Atlas. Teeth gritted, moving like a wink of lightning, Gabriel dug his shoulder into Atlas's stomach. As he slammed into the wall, Atlas looked at Gabriel with rage and shock. Then the CIA operative saw the Gurkha blade embedded in the table, less than a foot from his face.

Vic Gabriel was already tracking on. He found the savage face of the Gurkha warrior, now bladeless, and pumped a .44 slug into the guy's chest. Out of ammo, Gabriel snapped open the cylinder. Quickly, wishing to God that the Ruger Redhawk could handle speedloaders, he shoved three .44 cartridges into chambers, flicked the cylinder shut.

Boolewarke's merciless M60 assault pinned two more Russians to the wall, spreading their juices in gory arcs across the room. Venting his fury in a mad howl, the Dutchman kept triggering the M60, spraying those falling Ivans with a fusillade of 7.62mm NATO flesheaters and piledriving them into the floor.

Knowing they had to get the hell out of the opium den before a wall of crazed human flesh came tumbling down on them, Gabriel was leading the charge across the room. With a backhand hammerfist, he pulped a Newar's nose to scarlet mush.

"Keep moving, Vic! I got these Russian bastards! Christ's eyes, they're dead red meat!" Boolewarke yelled, raking the den with a hurricane of lead, kicking another Russian into the arms of Arabs and Mongols, the dead weight of that SPETSNAZ hitter sending the living wall of men reeling to the floor.

Johnny Simms spotted the sword, a flash of steel in the corner of his eye. Ducking, the black ex-merc felt the edge of the blade nearly part his scalp. He felt the blood run, wet and hot, down the side of his face. With fear-and-rage-powered might, Simms pistoned a sidekick into the breadbasket of the Mongol swordsman. The Mongol crumpled to his knees and vomited a stream of *rakshi*.

Wherever gunmetal showed, Boolewarke showered a hellstorm of lead over the mob.

The Gurkha knife slashed across Attila's back. Crying out, the Company operative nose-dived to the floor. He rolled over to squeeze off a round from his .45, but Zac

Dillinger was ventilating the Gurkha policeman with double-fisted Blood and Guts fury.

With a long burst from his M60, Boolewarke marched a line of 7.62mm flesheaters up the spine of the last Russian assassin. As that Russian hit the floor, sliding face-and belly-first in his own erupting gore, Gabriel, Simms, and Dillinger reached the foot of the steps. Turning, the three commandos watched as Attila and Atlas ran up to them.

"I thought Kathmandu was supposed to be a holy city?" Zac Dillinger rasped, ramming fresh 15-round clips into both .45 automatics. "I tell ya what, Kali, or Buddha or whoever, sure wasn't looking over these sinners today."

Grimly, Johnny Simms, blood streaming down the side of his face, looked back at the sea of dead. Limbs twitched in death throes. Blood pumped from gaping wounds in chests and backs.

"They're holy now, all right, Bad One. Real *holey.*"

"Let's get outta here!" Attila, the blood soaking into the side of his blacksuit, snarled. "Before the Gurkha cavalry arrives."

"Hey, man!" Simms called after Attila as the operative started up the steps.

"What?"

"I heard something earlier about believers. Was wondering if we made believers out of you?"

"Yeah, sure, I'm a believer," Attila growled back, his eyes fixed on the doorway at the top of the steps. "Just like the old Monkee record."

I got your Monkey, Vic Gabriel thought, ears ringing with the hollow roar of deafening silence—the aftermath of slaughter. *Right on my back. See no evil. Hear no evil. Speak no evil.*

As the few survivors gazed in fear and shock toward the doorway, Henry van Boolewarke backpedaled out of the opium den. The M60 was smoking in the Dutchman's hands.

Dark shadows, they trudged through the metallic light. A full moon beamed down over the glacier valley.

In both Russian and Nepali, SPETSNAZ commandos shouted at the Sherpa porters to move faster. Or die where they stood.

Under the threatening black eyes of AK-47s, the Sherpas lugged the rucksacks along. Occasionally, a Sherpa would stumble in a snowdrift. If he didn't rise immediately, Lieutenant General Mikhail Vishtka gave the order.

"*Nyet millosti!* No mercy! Kill the Mongol!"

And a sharp crack would echo throughout the valley. A valley of death.

Vishtka, an AK-47 slung around his shoulder, took up the rear. From there, he could spot any loafers, search for malcontents. Already, the trail that cut above the Arun Gorge was littered with six corpses of Mongols. After they were shot, the executioner would order the closest Mongol to toss the body into the gorge.

And Mikhail Vishtka was far from finished with the killing of his hated enemy, the ancient Mongols. There was honor, he believed, in shedding the blood of the accursed Tartars.

"Sergeant Jenenkov!" Vishtka called out, his voice carried to the point men by a wind that lashed at his back. Up front, Lieutenants Vorshilokov and Kuchenski flanked the porters, marching alongside the sergeant, constantly threatening any stragglers with death. "We set camp for the night at the edge of the platform."

"*Da*, Comrade Lieutenant General."

In the distance, the four Mi-24 Hinds were grounded on the platform, near the lower glacier that had fractured, eons ago, at the base of a two-thousand-foot ice face. Rotor blades throbbed out as they slowly spun to a stop, and commandos were disembarking from the gunships to make camp ready. During the day, the weather had held, and those gunships had scoured the face of the mountain for three hours, searching for any sign of life. They had found nothing.

The forced march was about to end. For the night.

They had already passed through the glacier valley, climbed several hundred meters up a slope that gradually inclined for the ice face. From there on, he knew it would be tough climbing. Up the crevasses of the glacier. Hammering pitons into the ice and rock, struggling, inch by inch, yard by yard up a sixty-five-degree face until a mantelshelf was reached.

Above, the SPETSNAZ lieutenant general heard the roar of the avalanche. He shivered as the icy winds blasted down from the mountain. Steep walls of rock hemmed the expedition force in. Surrounded them like silent, brooding sentinels, Vishtka reflected.

Vishtka trudged through the snow, moving up the line of Mongol porters. He wanted tents pitched and food served within twenty minutes. He was cold, hungry, and tired. He needed a good night's sleep so that he would be ready to break camp and begin the ascent, hours before daybreak. Equipment had to be weighed out, sorted, and divided up.

The ascent, *da*.

The final assault.

The evidence of CIA treachery, he knew, was higher up. Much, much higher up.

Then he heard it. A ferocious growl, then bone-chilling screams.

The sound of terror, as a man shrieked, froze Vishtka in his tracks for a heartbeat. Whirling, he saw the frenzied commotion in the rear. One of the porters was wrestling with something . . . a cat!

Snow leopard.

Frantically, Sherpa porters battered the snow leopard with their hands and feet. Finally, AK-47 autofire rang out. Slugs stitched the pale misty-gray coat of the snow leopard. The cat's long tail whipped into the snow as a hail of 7.62mm slugs spat up white puffs around the beast. The snow leopard's big paws seemed to grab at the air, as if it were desperately seeking to find some toehold on the ridge from which it had jumped to maul its victim.

Finally, the cat lay utterly still, the snow turning crimson as it soaked up the leopard's blood.

Stunned, the porters backed away from the snow leopard. Vishtka looked at the carcass. It was a big cat, more than a hundred pounds and six feet in length. A beautiful beast, Vishtka thought. Bold. Agile. Fearless. A true hunter. A warrior.

Then Vishtka looked at the snow leopard's victim. The porter was outstretched in the snow, facedown in a dark red splotch. With the toe of his boot, Vishtka rolled the body over. The snow leopard had torn the Mongol's throat out. There was nothing but a mass of ragged flesh and oozing blood where the man's throat had been. Vishtka felt nothing for the dead Sherpa. Now he just had one less mouth to worry about feeding.

Suddenly, Vishtka became aware of the babbling around him. The Mongols appeared frightened. Vishtka sensed the fear, hate, and rage in the icy air like a palpable force.

Sergeant Jenenkov was running up to Lieutenant General Vishtka.

"Sergeant!" Vishtka snapped. "What are they gibbering about?"

Vishtka saw the sergeant stop, heard him ask the khan, Timur Bhantaj, something in the Mongol tongue. Vishtka found himself hating the khan more and more as the hours passed. There was a quiet dignity about Timur Bhantaj that Vishtka distrusted. *Da*, there was vengeance in the khan's heart, Vishtka decided. At times, Vishtka could almost feel the khan's dark eyes boring into the backs of his commandos.

"Well, Sergeant?"

"The khan," Sergeant Jenenkov answered, "he says that death will follow more than just his own people. We have violated the throne of the mountain gods. He says when the snow leopard attacks it is an omen. He says the mountain gods are angry. There will be death ahead, he assures me."

"I am sure," Vishtka said to himself. "Assure the khan that he will be the first to die should something like this happen to one of our own. Move them out, Sergeant!"

As the commandos angrily urged the porters ahead, Vishtka held his ground. For a long moment, he stared at the dead Sherpa, then looked at the snow leopard.

The wind howled around Lieutenant General Mikhail Vishtka. The snow swirled in a mini-cyclone around the dark shadows on the plateau.

Vishtka shivered beneath his white windsuit. He let his hand wander over the red star on his breast, reflecting that he was on a great mission of justice for the motherland. He hadn't heard word yet from his agents in Kathmandu and he wondered if the foreigners had been found. He should have heard something hours ago. He was suddenly worried.

Something had gone wrong, he was sure. But what? Why was there no word from his people in Kathmandu?

As he looked up the jagged face of Mount Makalu, Vishtka experienced a stab of terror. He wondered what tomorrow would bring.

They were about to assault the Leviathan. He thought about the khan's words, and he realized just then that he was alone with Death.

The porters and the commandos were already nearing the gunships.

Makalu, he thought, and gazed skyward, searching for

the summit but seeing only darkness. *How does a man defeat something that doesn't even fight back?* Then again, he thought, listening to the moaning wind, feeling the snow sting his exposed face, perhaps the mountain doesn't need to fight at all. *Da*, perhaps the mountain simply lets man defeat himself.

Chapter 10

"Listen, soldier, how many times I gotta tell you people? How the hell should I know why those Russians showed up when they did?"

Until you make believers out of us, that's when, pal, Vic Gabriel thought, ignoring Atlas and stretching out in a prone position on the jagged lip of the ridge. Beside Gabriel, Simms, Dillinger, and Boolewarke took up their own surveillance positions, outstretched in the virgin snow on their bellies. They had reached the target valley, and Tamerlane was in sight. Through the stygian gloom, Gabriel spotted the yurts, perched on small hills that were cut into the valley like terraced steps. The Russians, Gabriel saw, had taken over the Sherpa village, sealed it off with gunmen in whitesuit. HK33 in hand, Gabriel looked at the grounded Antonovs. Lights shone in the open fuselage doors of the Soviet transport planes, and Gabriel made out the shadows of Russian commandos as they hung around the big birds or stood sentry duty near the yurts. Directly ahead, Gabriel spotted dozens of dark lumps, strewn across the pasture. The carcasses of yaks. Gabriel could still smell the blood in the air.

It was going to be a night for killing, he knew.

North, a giant black wall of rock, the Himalayas, loomed over Tamerlane, jagging into a clear velvet sky. A fifteen-hundred-mile curve of granite, he thought, that would hem in one ugly bitch of a showdown. East meets

111

West. The Eagle and the Bear. The time had come, yeah. The time to draw second blood. SPETSNAZ blood.

It had been a long, hard ten-hour drive across rugged country, and Vic Gabriel found his nerves becoming dangerously frayed from impatience. Snaking the jeep through snow-drenched trails. Skirting the edge of a gorge. Passing beyond Sherpa villages. Worried about Gurkha patrols. Digging the jeep out of a snowdrift, not once, but three times. Time was, indeed, killing them, Gabriel thought.

Because the opium den had been well below ground, a vault where the underbelly of Kathmandu crawled in the sludge of their vices, Eagle Force and the CIA operatives had been able to beat a hasty but unopposed retreat from Kathmandu. Luckily, the sounds of the furious battle waged in the opium den had not carried beyond the heavy steel doors to the streets of Kathmandu, or Gabriel believed that they might all be sitting in a cell right now, hoping Uncle Sam would bail them out. Even still, Attila had kept his so-called "papers" ready, just in case they were stopped by Gurkhas. During the drive, Boolewarke, a qualified paramedic, had sewn more than thirty stitches in Attila's back. Carefully shaving Simms's bloody scalp with a straightedge razor, the Dutchman had also stitched up the ugly gash along the top of the black ex-merc's head. They were both hurting, and there was a good chance those sutures would tear open in the hours ahead, Gabriel knew. But every man now had to be ready to go. And expect the worst.

Tamerlane was first on the hit list. The Russians, Gabriel knew, had to be dislodged from the Sherpa village. Dislodged by Death.

Or the hunters could become the hunted.

"Can we put the nasty little insinuations behind us and get down to the business of killing?" Attila growled, wincing as he showed signs of the pain from his injury, his gloved hands wrapped around an M-16 with an M203 grenade launcher. "I'm getting tired of you people acting like we're a couple of BAs."

"BAs?" Simms queried.

"Benedict Arnolds," Attila said.

Boolewarke was togged in combat whitesuit like the other commandos, his webbing fitted with a mix of fragmentation and incendiary grenades. The Dutchman had mounted an infrared scope on his favored Barnett Panzer crossbow for the nighthit. "This whole operation's turned nasty, chum," he said gruffly. "It suits my mood just fine. So let me whisper some words of wisdom to ya. Let it be. Or let it BA."

"Stuck with four fuckin' comedians, bad ones, I might add," Atlas grumbled, his own M-16 with attached M203 grenade launcher strapped around his shoulder.

"Till Death do us part," Johnny Simms muttered.

Gabriel looked back down the hill, searched the snow-carpeted plain beyond. "When are those porters of yours going to show up, Attila? Maybe your *sirdar* got cold feet? Maybe you didn't shell out enough rupees or tugriks or whatever to make him want to risk his ass for Uncle Sam?"

"How come I gotta keep repeating myself with you people?" Attila growled. "Look, soldier, I already told you, they were pulled back another five klicks when SPETSNAZ dropped in and told to sit tight until they heard from me. You heard me radio the *sirdar* from Kathmandu and tell 'em to move out and link up with us here. In this snow, lugging along all that gear, it'll take them some time to get here by foot, I would imagine."

"We ain't got time, bubba," Johnny Simms said, peering over the ridgeline. "And we sure ain't got time to be imaginin' nothin'. Ivan's got a full day's head start by now."

"Ivan's also got to pitch camp . . . bubba," Attila said.

"Which means we've got to hike through the night to gain some ground, no matter how dangerous it might be," Atlas pointed out.

"All right, but first we've got to get by our buddies on the yak pasture," Gabriel said. "Dutch, take the high ground to the north. Move down and let the arrows fly—you know the routine," he said, checking his Rolex. "Fifteen minutes will give us time enough to crawl through the yak dung and move in on those Antonovs."

"Hey, whose giving the orders here?" Attila rasped.

But Henry van Boolewarke was already sliding off into the darkness, vanishing as he crouched below the ridgeline to take up his offensive position.

"I'd like to make this a quiet hit," Gabriel said, "but there's no telling how many Russians are in those yurts. If we're lucky, they'll be stuffing their faces with *tsampa,* and maybe sampling some of the Mongol women on this cold winter night. All right, Atlas, I'm throwing the ball to you. Call it. Quiet or noisy?"

Silently, Atlas chewed over the situation for a second, fingering his mustache. "Take 'em as they come, and kill 'em where they stand. You and the P.I. can move in. Simms can man the .50-caliber in the jeep and I'll take the M60 on the passenger's side."

"That leaves Attila the Hun here with the chauffeur duties," Simms remarked, and Attila flashed the black ex-merc a dark look.

Gabriel slipped his arm through the HK33's strap, unsheathed his commando dagger, stood, and moved away from the ridge. "Let's roll, then, people. And oh, yeah," the ex-CIA assassin said over his shoulder, hitting the snow on his belly, a wry smile ghosting his lips. "I'm a believer."

Attila looked at Atlas, puzzled. "What the hell's that supposed to mean?"

"It means Gabriel thinks he's a big hotshot, that's what."

"Hotshot, my ass," Attila muttered as Atlas stood and shadowed down the slope behind Johnny Simms.

"It's a short ride, Colonel. It's always a short ride—when you're on the other side of the tracks. This is where you get off."

And Vic Gabriel meant it. From the bottom of a heart hardened by the sickness of a world gone mad. For those like Colonel Nelson, he believed, the short ride could only take them into one place. Oblivion.

Nelson gritted his teeth in agony. "Short ride? You wanna talk about short rides? Take a look at what's happening down here, mister. Take a look at the rest of the world. The whole human race is sitting right on top of a time bomb. Don't you understand? Can't you see it? You take what you can get in life, and you hope that by taking some you can put yourself in a position to give back and make a difference. So why don't you wake up and smell your own moralizing bullshit? Sometimes, to win, you've got to give in a little to the other side. Bend the rules enough so that you're in a position to win."

"I'm wide-awake, Colonel. You used me, Colonel. To get your cocaine and to bring Alvarez back alive, most likely so you could work him over, make some deal with him. If he didn't deal . . . well, we all know the end of that story. I suppose if something went wrong I was going to take the fall in your place. Yeah, I'm wide-awake all right, Colonel. And my eyes have rolled back in my head, more than once, to see inside and wonder what this madness all is. I understand that Latin America is AFU. But who's to blame? The Incas for letting the Spanish wipe them off the face of the earth? The Spanish, for setting themselves up on a deposed Inca throne? The Spanish in Latin America, Colonel, are headed in the same direction as the Incas.

You see, Colonel, history should be mankind's greatest—hell, its only—bona fide teacher. The names, the places change, the firepower changes. But one thing and one thing only remains constant and unchangeable—human nature. We bend to the right, but we're not willing to break completely free of that darkness in our hearts.

"I've seen that communism can't and won't work. Because of human nature. I see that democracy has little hope left. Because of human nature. The only hope for democracy, Colonel, is to keep guys like you out of the game. And in the end, it's all a game, Colonel, isn't it? The most serious game going. The game of life and death. The game of surviving. Because, I believe, it doesn't just end here. If it did, then men could feel free to do whatever the hell it is they please. But there's always that voice inside you, Colonel. That voice that will give you a kind of warm feeling that you're on the right path, or a voice that will make you feel uncomfortable and squirm around in your own shit. You can listen to that voice, or you can choose to ignore it. There's a reason for right and wrong, Colonel, a reason for laws, even if they are man's laws, and even if you feel like they're wrong and shouldn't possibly apply to you. Those laws are there to keep human nature in line, Colonel, to try and maintain a balance between the light and the dark. You fucked with the balance, Colonel. You fucked up, big-time.

"You're right about one thing, though—the world is sitting right on top of a time bomb. I know I can't defuse that bomb—completely. But I can slow down the fire igniting that fuse. And yeah, I hope, too. I hope that I can and will make some difference. I hope that I can buy the good guys some time." Gabriel jerked a nod at the crates. "This shit, though, whatever your reason for trafficking in it, isn't the answer. It's ruin. It's innocent-looking enough, but that's the illusion. All you're doing is feeding the fuse to that bomb. All you're doing is feeding your own special

*kind of addiction. Power. Grandiosity. You're a little ty-
rant, looking to move up. Just what did you think you're
going to do for Latin America, Colonel? Is this going to
help the contras? Is this going to stabilize a Latin American economy already shattered and decimated because of
the kind of greed and chaos this ruin brings? Does everybody live happily ever after when you move this shit?"*

Nelson clenched his jaw. He sat in stony silence, his
rasping breath penetrating the crackling of nearby flames.

"You don't see it, do you? You don't want to see it, do
you?" Vic Gabriel nodded. "And so it goes, Colonel. It's all
a stage down here. Latin America keeps pumping this shit
out and poisoning Uncle Sam. While Uncle Sam keeps
pumping big dollars into Latin America. Uncle Sam's
banks have a huge lobby force in the District of Clowns.
Nobody is allowed to make any kind of move because those
banks want their money back. And so it goes. Around and
around. And guys like me? We're stuck right in the middle
of a crossfire hurricane. Tugged and blown in each direction. Wondering if we're going to fall through the cracks
ourselves. Hoping against hope that we can slow that fuse
down. But this guy, he doesn't get tugged easy, Colonel.
You fucked with the bull by grabbing its horns and you got
gored. Me, I know it can't even be fucked with."

Nelson's expression suddenly went slack. His eyes
glazed over with thought for a moment, then he looked at
Gabriel with renewed conviction.

"Listen, Gabriel, you know how much money is there?"

"It's not chump change, Colonel, that much I know. I
figure you could probably move it and end up with enough
money to buy a small country in Latin America. To be
moving this kind of weight, I figured you and Alvarez had
some pretty heavy connections."

"Listen, don't go off half-cocked here," Nelson im-
plored. "I'm connected, damn right. First of all, you take
me out, you'll be looking over your shoulder the rest of

117

*your very short life. You wanna talk about short rides?
You won't get out of the starting gate if you take me down.
I'm trying to reason with you, mister. All right, I can
respect and appreciate your point of view—up to a reason-
able point. So let's talk reason here.*

"I'm sitting on big-time weight there. Three hundred
and fifty keys to be exact. That's only the beginning.
That's my foot in the door. I can move that stuff at thirty
big ones a key, wholesale. I cut it, I can triple my profit,
and no one will even know the difference. In six months, I
can be moving the stuff by the ton. What do you think
you're going to do anyway? You gonna stop it, a one-man
army? That shit only works in the movies. In reality, pal,
the good guys very seldom win. In reality, the good guys
often become the bad guys."

"So I've learned."

"So you've learned? Learn this, mister. I'm trying to
cut you in, I'm giving you a viable option here and all you
wanna do is play hard guy. Hard guys get castrated, pal.
You learn to survive, you learn to get along, because by
getting along you can move along."

"To what?"

Nelson was silent for a moment. "To what?"

Gabriel's eyes flickered over the discarded AutoMag,
which was less than four feet away from Nelson. He
started to lower the .45 Detonics, hoping against hope.

Because this was the end of the line for Nelson.

"No deal. I'll take my chances," Gabriel said. "I kinda
like the way that voice in my head is now. Now, here's my
deal, Colonel. You come back to the States with me. You
give me some names. You—"

A maniacal rage twisted Nelson's face. Screaming,
Nelson scooped up the AutoMag.

Gabriel had hoped against hope that Nelson would at
least consider another option. Foolish hope. The problem
with the monster inside is that once it digs its claws into

you, it doesn't want to let go. Death is the only thing the monster knows, because death is the reality of the illusion. You feed the monster because you yourself want death, Vic Gabriel knew. You feed the monster, hoping it will give back some of the everything it has taken from you. But it never does. It simply devours you.

Triggering his Detonics, Gabriel pumped a .45 slug into the meaty part of Nelson's thigh. Two long strides and Gabriel kicked the AutoMag out of Nelson's hand, sending the cannon spinning through the fuselage doorway.

"One last chance, Colonel."

"Fuck you!"

"Suit yourself."

Gun trained on Nelson's mask of agony, Gabriel dug his hand into the colonel's shoulder and dragged him across the floorboard. Dumping the colonel in front of his crates, Gabriel found a weapons bin in the aft. M-16 assault rifles, some Uzis, spare clips. And an MK2 frag grenade.

"What are you doing?" Nelson snarled, an edge of fear in his voice.

MK2 in hand, Gabriel backed up toward the cockpit.

"This has a four-second delay, Colonel. I'm giving you your last viable option. I figure you can reach this grenade a full second before it blows." Gabriel pulled the pin but didn't release the spoon. "You reach the grenade you have three choices. Throw it behind me. Or throw it to the left, away from you and me. Or just sit on it. It's your decision. Now, I won't guarantee that I'll just quietly go to my own death if you choose the first option. Decision time, Colonel. Pick one. Life. Death. Or take your chances with oblivion."

Releasing the spoon, Gabriel dropped the grenade on the floorboard, hopped out of the gunship.

One.

Gun low by his side, Gabriel strode away from the gunship, his head cocked sideways.

Two.

Fear and rage contorted Nelson's face. His breath shot out of his mouth in a ragged rasp. For a split second he stared at the grenade, just several feet away.

"Y-you . . ."

Desperately, Nelson crabbed across the floorboard. A strange whimpering sound choked in Nelson's throat. He fisted the grenade.

Three.

Vic Gabriel turned, saw the shadow in the fuselage kneel up. A wild glow lit Nelson's eyes as he held the grenade.

"You cocksucking mother—"

Vic Gabriel looked away as the ball of fire vaporized Colonel Nelson and ripped through the gunship.

Vic Gabriel kept looking away and he didn't look back as he headed for the jeep.

Colonel Nelson made his own decision.

Oblivion.

"And let there be darkness," Vic Gabriel muttered to himself.

And he wondered if the dead could hear him.

Take them as they come. Kill them where they stand.

Atlas's words of grim wisdom rang through Gabriel's head as he crawled through the snow, closing down on the tail of the Antonov. There was an itch, right between Gabriel's shoulder blades, the same itch he got every time he felt his backside wasn't covered. Without a doubt his commandos were reliable, but he had some serious reservations about Atlas and Attila. He couldn't help but believe that Atlas wasn't just talking about the Russians when he had spoken those cryptic words. *In the end, it always comes down to every man for himself anyway.*

Gabriel, crabbing through the snow, stopped and checked his Rolex. He had less than three minutes to take out the first sentry, knew Boolewarke must now be in position somewhere in the hills, his crossbow loaded with a broadhead arrow ready to fly. Less than ten meters ahead, Gabriel's first target stood in the fuselage doorway of the Antonov. The Russian was puffing on a *machorka*, stargazing. This hit required pistols with silencers, and Gabriel found himself cursing his decision to go with hand cannons as sidearms. The Ka-Bar and garrote would have to do. In the distance, sitting between the other two Antonovs, was the ZSU-23-4 antiaircraft battery. The multiple barrels were aimed skyward, and three sentries were roving around the ZSU-23-4, ready to man the multiple-barreled cannon at the first hint of trouble from above. Elsewhere, Gabriel counted nine enemy numbers around Tamerlane. The village was as silent, as dark as the Himalayas.

Then something happened that Vic Gabriel hadn't counted on.

Dillinger jabbed Gabriel in the calf with the handle of his Ka-Bar. Intently, Gabriel followed Dillinger's fear-cut gaze. Gabriel heard the faint whir.

Large square objects flanked the ZSU-23-4. A round object was now slowly rising from those box-shaped structures. Before the floodlights flashed on in a blazing glare that lit the yak pasture up like the Fourth of July, Gabriel knew they were in serious trouble. Whether by accident or design, and Gabriel didn't know nor care at the moment, the floodlights were sweeping over the pasture.

"They'll see us for sure!" Dillinger hissed through clenched teeth. "A foot of snow won't cover our big fat asses, VG. We'll stand out like a couple of yetis!"

The white beams of light roved toward Gabriel and Dillinger.

"Might as well start it now, Zac!" Gabriel rasped. "I

don't think Ivan will let us just throw our hands up and ask for mercy in this situation. The abominable snowman doesn't carry around an assault rifle."

"Mercy never entered my mind."

"Nor mine. Drop the bastards where they stand!"

Sheathing their Ka-Bars, Gabriel and Dillinger unslung their HK33s.

And not a second too soon.

Gabriel heard the shouted warning as the searchlights washed over them. Up and running toward the yak carcasses, Gabriel and Dillinger triggered their HK33s on full-auto. The Ivan with the *machorka* in his mouth was ventilated by a quick burst from Gabriel's chattering HK33, a stream of 5.56x45mm slugs ripping apart the red star on his chest, flinging him back into the fuselage.

Firing on the run, Dillinger and Gabriel stitched two more Russians standing outside the fuselage of another Antonov. Then slugs began peppering the snow around the two commandos in a searing lead hurricane. Before nose-diving behind the yak carcasses, Gabriel saw one of the SPETSNAZ commandos beside the ZSU-23-4 pitch to the ground, the Russian's hands grabbing at the arrow impaled in his chest.

The doors to three yurts burst open and six more Russians with AK-47s crouched in doorways. Russian voices, yelling and cursing. And there was fear in those voices.

Gabriel blinded the searchlights with two 3-round bursts, shattering glass and bathing the pasture in darkness. Even still, a rain of ComBloc lead ripped into the snow around Gabriel and Dillinger, and yak carcasses were pulverized by the Russian return barrage.

Snow stinging his face, chunks of bloody yak hide pelting his body, Gabriel knew they were pinned down. And in serious trouble.

Pencil-tip flames were stabbing through the darkness. From the ZSU-23-4 antiaircraft battery. From the fuselage doorways of the Antonovs. From the doorways of the yurts.

The air was blistered by autofire, and Gabriel felt the slipstream of hot lead as it tore past him.

"Christ, Ivan must've left two full fucking squads behind!" Dillinger yelled over the din of autofire, the ex-P.I. and Gabriel flinching as a relentless hellstorm of 7.62mm lead churned up the carcasses around them, a thudding meat grinder. "Where's our relief, anyway!"

Another SPETSNAZ commando tumbled away from the ZSU-23-4 Quad cannon, an arrowpoint jutting from the side of his neck.

Through the roar of autofire, Gabriel made out the grind of an engine. Twisting his head sideways, he saw the jeep, flying over the edge of the ridge, a second later.

"Spell that S-I-M-M-S!" Gabriel answered.

Spewing fine clouds of snow in its wake, the jeep raced past Gabriel and Dillinger. Craning himself out the passenger-side window, Atlas let the M60 rip. As the jeep jounced over yak carcasses, surged past Antonovs one and two, Johnny Simms triggered the .50-caliber machine. An angry tongue of flame shot out from the bed of the jeep as Simms churned the Russians in the doorways of the Antonovs up with the big maneater, slugs screaming off metal, *thwacking* off hunks of flesh, and driving Marxist-Leninists back into the bowels of the transport planes.

Using the suppressing fire from the armored jeep to cover their advance, Gabriel and Dillinger bolted for the closest Antonov. A line of slugs drilled into the snow on their heels, then Gabriel triggered a short burst at the Russian shooting for glory for the motherland and sent the Marxist killer reeling away from the nose of the Antonov, blood erupting from that Ivan's chest and stomach in dark scarlet fountain-fingers. From between the next two Antonovs, Gabriel heard the sharp cry, then spotted the

Russian as he crumpled to his knees, his hands clutching at the arrow shaft protruding from his chest.

Just as he thought the tide of battle was washing back in their favor, Gabriel, hitting a combat crouch beside the fuselage of the Antonov, heard a familiar sound. Listening to the night, he heard the throb of rotor blades.

Dillinger looked at Gabriel, cursed. "One of our Ivan buddies radioed for help."

Scouring the black sky, Gabriel saw the gunship soar over the black plugs of sawtooth rock to the northwest. Nosedown, the Mi-24 was zeroing in on Tamerlane. The white-camouflage job on the gunship, Gabriel noted, made the bird stand out in the night like a giant snowball. That didn't mean it was any less deadly, Gabriel knew.

"That was quick," Gabriel said. "The rest of the SPETSNAZ force must be closer than we thought. Or maybe the Marxist fly-boys were doing a little night recon."

"That's great! Now where's our Spooky when we need it to take care of our Russian Red Barons, huh?" Dillinger growled. "Where's our big air fire support, tell me that?"

"Probably sitting on a private airstrip in Thailand by now," Gabriel answered. "Loading up a few thousand bricks of heroin!"

"Naw, the Company wouldn't do that," Dillinger dryly remarked, then ducked as a slug screamed off the fuselage above his head.

Like some great bird of prey, the Mi-24 swooped over Tamerlane. Gabriel held his breath, hoped for the best, but knew the worst was coming.

Fire blazed from the nose of the Mi-24 as the gunship opened up on the armored jeep with its 12.7mm minigun typhoon.

The worst began to hammer down upon Eagle Force. With a vengeance.

Chapter 11

The gunship seemed to appear out of nowhere, a white specter, a lethal blot against the Makalu massif. And Johnny Simms knew they were all in trouble.

Potential death came blazing over the village from above, and a gale force barrage of 12.7mm slugs was pounding into the armored hull of the jeep. Simms held on to the .50-caliber maneater, riding out the recoil for all he was worth. Shells spitting off the wall of the bed around his face with a fury, the black ex-merc nearly cut a Russian, firing at the jeep from the doorway of a yurt, in half. As the jeep sluiced for a sideways run at the antiaircraft battery, Simms directed his relentless machine gun fire at three Ivans blazing away at Gabriel and Dillinger. Their HK33s spewing lead, Gabriel and Dillinger nailed those three Russians to the fuselage of an Antonov. Simms helped to further tear the Russians apart with a steady fusillade, and those Russians were scythed into bursting sacks of gore. Dancing in death down the fuselage of the transport plane, and yeah, quite dead before they hit the blood-soaked snow.

Right then, Simms experienced a strange and perverse kind of exhilaration. Jungle warfare was stealth and cunning, stalking the enemy through the bush, never knowing who or what would turn up before there was even a chance to react to a threat. Now, here in the valley of Tamerlane, Simms was face-to-face with a new kind of warfare.

Open warfare.

Head-to-head.

Now, he thought, combatants were going for broke. Upfront. Eyeball-to-eyeball. *No skulking through the bushes bullshit*.

"Slow it down!"

Simms twisted around. The whole damn jeep was rocking under the roaring rain of 12.7mm lead, the white-camoued Mi-24 bearing down on a straight line toward the vehicle. Within seconds, Simms knew that the gunship would be right on top of them. Would probably hover and cut loose with several rockets that would spatter them halfway across Nepal.

Sweeping his M-16 off the floorboard, Atlas thrust himself through the door. He hit the snow, rolling. A line of slugs raked the snow, stitching a line toward the CIA operative. Grim-faced, Atlas knelt. Like a block of stone, Atlas held his ground, the jeep sliding away in a spume of snow, leaving the operative exposed to the tracking line of 12.7mm minigun fire. On his own, staring up into the eye of Death, Atlas was fused for a brief second behind a rapidly thinning cloud of snow.

In disbelief, Johnny Simms watched as Atlas hefted the M-16 with the attached M203, placed the stock against his shoulder.

Crazy bastard! Simms thought, the warbird streaking right at Atlas.

Atlas triggered the M203 a millisecond before 12.7mm slugs ripped into him.

Atlas cried out, pitched to the ground, the M-16 flying from his grasp.

The 40mm hellbomb slammed into the nose of the Mi-24.

Side by side, their HK33s poised to fire, Vic Gabriel and Zac Dillinger watched as the gunship erupted into a ball of flames, a flash of fire that burned across the sky.

Attila braked the jeep, burst out onto the killing field, M-16 in hand.

Twisted, fiery wreckage seared through the darkness. The fireball blazed, seemed suspended in the sky for an eternal second. Finally, hulks of debris pounded to the snow.

Simms, fisting his own HK33, vaulted out of the jeep's bed.

Eagle Force rolled into mop-up detail.

Quickly, they checked the Antonovs, then the yurts for Russian stragglers. Checked the Russian dead for any possums. One horribly wounded Russian was treated to a quick mercy burst from Dillinger's HK33.

Minutes later, satisfied that the Russians had been erased from Tamerlane, Gabriel and his commandos gathered around Atlas. Staring down at Atlas, Gabriel saw the pearly-white strands of guts seeping through the splayed fingers of the operative. The guy had iron balls; Gabriel had to give him that much.

"The yurts are clean," Simms informed Gabriel. "Just women and children and a handful of old men."

And those women, children, and old men now ventured outside their yurts.

Attila walked up to Eagle Force.

Fiery wreckage crackled around Gabriel.

The snow crimson wet around him, Atlas coughed, spat up blood. There was a glazed look in the operative's eyes, and Gabriel knew he wouldn't last but a few minutes longer. And that was stretching it.

Without hesitation, Attila pumped a 3-round burst into Atlas's chest. Simms flinched at the sudden stutter of weapons fire.

Gabriel pinned Attila with an icy stare. "He might've

made it," he said, even though he knew that wasn't true. Still, he was gauging Attila.

"Bullshit," Attila rasped. "I got my orders. Wounded weight is dead weight. Remember that, soldier."

Gabriel was about to tell Attila he would *remember that* when the operative stared right past him. Turning, Gabriel saw the dark shadows trudging over the ridgeline. As the group headed across the yak pasture, Gabriel made out the rucksacks, the rope, and climbing gear.

"Looks like your *sirdar*, Attila," Dillinger said gruffly, then slapped a fresh 30-round clip into his HK33. "I guess it's time to assault Makalu and pray the mountain gods don't shit all over us."

"I don't want any more than a dozen porters, Attila, you understand?" Gabriel said.

"And why's that?"

"Take a look around you, that's why," Gabriel answered. "I don't need their wounded weight on my conscience. Go talk to them. Don't give me any crap, because you're outnumbered now four to one, and I'm not dancing around with you anymore. *Remember that*. Johnny, Zac, let's go through those Antonovs and see what we can scrounge up."

Attila said nothing for a moment, then muttered an oath to himself.

"Jesus bloody Christ! Bloody Buddha! Kali's fuck!"

Gabriel saw Boolewarke slide through the darkness near the Antonovs, the crossbow gripped in the Dutchman's hands.

"What a fine mess we're locked into, eh, Victor?" the Dutchman rumbled. "Russian warbirds, SPETSNAZ assassins, and now these guys!" he said, jerking a nod at the band of Sherpa porters. "Sherpas, eh! Look more like something right out of twelfth-century Mongolia! A bloody Golden Horde! Buddha's eyes, what a bloody fuckin' mess!"

"You got that right, Dutch," the ex-CIA assassin said, heading toward the Antonovs. "And it's going to get messier, bet your ass."

"Hey!" Attila called out.

"Hey, what?" Gabriel barked over his shoulder, slinging the HK33 around his shoulder, sidestepping a Russian corpse.

"I need a hand with that ZSU."

"What for?"

"To clean up, that's what for."

"You hired a *sirdar* and porters," Gabriel flung back. "Use 'em."

Attila said nothing. Then he spat into the snow.

Bloody snow.

Fire crackled from the gunship wreckage.

Atlas's arm twitched once.

Attila cleaned up, all right. In grand Hun style, Vic Gabriel thought, watching as the operative unleashed the ZSU-23-4 Quad self-propelled AA gun.

Operated by valve-tech fire control, the quadruple cannon boomed out a furious wave of 23mm shells. A stream of shells pounded into the fuselages of the Antonovs, raking the transport planes in a raging firestorm of explosions. Each barrel hurling shells in 50-round bursts, the Soviet transport planes were pulped to flaming junk within seconds. The Sherpa porters and the Tamerlane villagers, huddled together in the icy night air near Gabriel and Eagle Force, watched the destruction with a mix of fear and grim fascination. And relief. The Soviet beast, Gabriel sensed, was being dealt payback. Vicious blows that would soon sever the head of the Russian hydra that had invaded their village.

Attila stood near the ZSU-23-4. The porters had helped the operative move the Quad cannon away from the Antonovs fifteen minutes ago. The cannons were set on auto, and all that was left to do now was wait until the last shells were spewed into the hellstorm.

"He didn't waste no time, did he?" Dillinger said in a loud voice, standing next to Gabriel, as the din of cannon fire pealed over the valley.

Huge twisted sheets of metal hurricaned across the yak pasture. Tremendous explosions geysered skyward on roiling tongues of fire. A full minute later, the pulverizing was over.

The cannons smoked.

The wind soughed through the flames, fanning the fires of destruction.

Attila trudged through the snow, fire belching across the yak pasture and wreckage slamming to snowy earth behind the operative.

The pilfering of the Antonovs had paid off for Gabriel and his commandos. They had taken two 7.62mm SVD sniper rifles from one of the transport planes, and four RPG-7 rocket launchers. A crate of 85mm warheads for the RPGs had been found in the aft of an Antonov, and *Sirdar* Amaka had eagerly accepted the task of hauling the crate. No, the Sherpa porters, Gabriel could tell, weren't about to be left out in the cold on this killhunt for the Russians. And since it was obvious they were intent on fighting alongside the commandos and not just hiking to haul supplies and equipment, Gabriel had stripped the Russian dead of AK-47s and several 7.62mm RPK light machine guns, and passed out almost two dozen RGD-5 fragmentation grenades among the Sherpas.

As Attila neared Eagle Force, Simms asked, "What was the point to all that? You just like noise, or what?"

"Figure it out for yourself, soldier," Attila growled, M-16 slung around his shoulder. "Ivan isn't going home. And if he makes it back here, there won't be any hasty retreat. Are you people stupid, or do you just like hearing yourselves ask questions?"

Eagle Force ignored Attila.

Ivan isn't going home. No hasty retreat. Okay, that made sense of Gabriel. What didn't make sense was the brutal way in which Attila had executed Atlas. Quick. Cold. No remorse. Like the guy didn't mean a damn thing once he'd bitten the snow in his own blood, even though he'd blown that Mi-24 out of the sky and saved their asses from getting chewed up and spread over the yak pasture in big chunks. Probably saved the whole damn village. Gabriel would keep a hard eye on Attila from there on out. Suddenly, he trusted the operative about as far as he could spit.

Another problem had arisen before the Antonovs were churned up into flaming scrap. The son of the village khan, young Karzim Bhantaj, had insisted to Attila that he be allowed to go with the commandos into the valley and up the slopes of Makalu. When Gabriel had objected, *Ang* Bhantaj had told Attila that his father was among the slaves doing the Russians' bidding. Bhantaj's people had been slaughtered by the Russian wild beasts, the young man said, his people enslaved. There was a blood debt to be repaid. Honor called for vengeance. And *Ang* Bhantaj claimed that he would simply follow the commandos and their porters if he was forced to stay behind. Because he didn't need a lone warrior in search of vengeance screwing up the killhunt from the rear, Gabriel had relented. Trouble was everywhere anyway, and Death was licking its greedy lips in hunger, Gabriel thought. Any way it was hacked, there was going to be a body count on Makalu. If *Ang* Bhantaj wanted some Russian blood . . . well, Gabriel decided to let it be.

Ang Bhantaj stood near Gabriel. He was dressed in a Mongol *kalat*, the tunic of his ancestors, wrapped in fur and armor. His quiver was stuffed with arrows and his bow was slung around his shoulder. Gabriel recognized the vengeance in the young Sherpa's eyes, indeed, could sympathize with Karzim. Hell, his own father had died at the treacherous hands of an enemy years ago. If he could have done something to prevent his father's death back then, Gabriel would have been right there in the eye of the fire, fighting by his father's side. Of course, he was grandstanding it now, looking back in anger and simply pissing in the wind. But maybe young Karzim could help save his own father. Maybe the boy felt he was owed that much by the commandos in return for Sherpa muscle. Gabriel felt his heart go out to *Ang* Bhantaj. Compassion aside, Gabriel had already told Attila to warn the young man that he would follow their orders at all times. The first sign of disobedience, and Gabriel would send Karzim back to Tamerlane.

Eagle Force stood ready, weapons strapped around their shoulders. The Sherpa porters, though they appeared nervous to Gabriel, looked set to embark on the manhunt, too.

"You know that when they don't hear from their fly-boys, SPETSNAZ will be expecting us," Gabriel told Attila. "Maybe even be waiting to ambush us."

"Tell me something I don't know, soldier. Let's hit the trail."

Attila brushed past Gabriel.

Lieutenant Kuchenski removed the radio headset. "Still no word from our pilot, Comrade Lieutenant General."

Chort vozmi! Worried, Vishtka began barking orders at his commandos and his Mongol porters. It was time to break camp, even though dawn was still close to four hours away. Gear was to be separated immediately. *Da*, he knew it would be dangerous climbing the icy crevasse in the dark, but he had no choice. Headlamps would light the way.

Something was wrong. They were being tracked. Worse still, they were being hunted by an unknown enemy. Most likely hunted, he thought, by CIA gangsters. CIA *kalorshniks*, criminals. *Chort!* His team of assassins had obviously failed him in Kathmandu. Their failure, he knew, was his failure. He would be held accountable by Moskva for every dead commando. Unless, of course, he succeeded. In locating the wreckage and extracting the mission recorders from the reconnaissance planes. And in killing the unknown enemy.

"Sergeant Jenenkov," Vishtka said, moving toward the grounded gunships. "You are to take one full squad. Find and position yourself in a crevasse once camp is cleared. Place a sentry at the other edge of the platform. The enemy will have to come this way. Once the enemy is spotted, that sentry will alert you. Wrap your weapons, bury yourselves beneath the snow and let the enemy pass you. We will move up the slope, move out onto the ice face, and position ourselves up there, somewhere on a ledge. I want all three Mi-24s airborne in two hours. I want the face scoured as high as the weather permits and then some, and I want that wreckage found. I must know how high we must climb! *Ponimayo, tovaritsch?*"

"*Da.* And the Sherpas?"

"They will come with us. There is to be no sign of our camp here. Whatever food and supplies we don't take with us are to be buried at base camp here. I have a feeling we must confront our hunters here on the glacier before any higher ascent is attempted."

Sergeant Jenenkov wheeled to carry out the orders.

His pulse racing with anxiety, his heart like a block of ice in his chest, Vishtka stared up the dark ice face. A two-thousand-foot ascent. What was up there and beyond? More rock, more ice, and more climbing, he knew. Aerial reconnaissance had spotted a ledge, two hundred meters up from where he now stood. *Da,* Vishtka thought, something they could climb out on and wait in hiding from above for the enemy to show. First, they would have to climb up the series of crevasses that spined the slope. Topping the crevasses, they could mount the ice face and find a ledge suitable for an ambush. It would take hours of grueling climbing, perhaps even take the rest of the day. But time was all Lieutenant General Vishtka had. Time to kill, *da*, he cryptically thought, and suppressed the smile.

Then the lieutenant general heard the rumble from high above.

Avalanche. Roaring again in all its primeval fury.

Chapter 12

"C'mon, move it. We don't have time to stop and smell the goddamn rhododendrons. That's a dead snow leopard, shot to shit," Attila growled, kicking at the carcass. "And that's a Sherpa with his throat torn out."

Crouched beside the bullet-riddled carcass, Vic Gabriel looked up at Attila. The guy showed him an ugly grin, then walked away, forging ahead into the howling wind and the light snowfall that fused the expedition force in a swirling sheet.

"A real compassionate fellow there, eh, Victor?" the Dutchman said, tugging his fur-lined hood closer to his face as he moved past Gabriel. With the Barnett Panzer crossbow slung around Boolewarke's shoulder, a Sherpa lugged the M60 machine gun and 7.62mm belt-links for the Afrikaner.

Rucksacks and weapons strapped around their shoulders, the porters trudged past Gabriel. Under Attila's threatening stare, the Sherpas didn't allow themselves but a second to view the dead.

"Couple thousand dollars of high-tech nylon and rubber," Johnny Simms griped, "and the wind and the cold are still carving a chunk outta my ass."

MM1 multiround projectile launcher slung around his shoulder, HK33 in his hands, Zac Dillinger replied, "Another thousand feet up, Johnny Boy, and you won't have any ass left to carve in this weather. Christ, it's cold! I can feel my balls shrivelin' right up into my bowels."

Freezing cold, right. Gabriel couldn't help but agree with Dillinger on that point. They had climbed steadily up the trail through the night, moving out of the Arun Gorge, and were now a little more than eight hours into the day. The air grew rapidly colder, and like knives, the wind seemed to slash at them.

Still kneeling beside the carcass, Gabriel looked ahead, then skyward. A low cloud bank hung over the valley glacier, and the snowflakes seemed to grow larger before Gabriel's eyes with each passing minute. Visibility was damn near zero. If the weather worsened, they would have to stop. Everything appeared gray on white to Gabriel.

But the ex-CIA assassin's heart was black with mounting anxiety, his combat senses on full alert.

Vic Gabriel sensed they were going to have to stop soon anyway. And not because of nature.

Because of animal man.

Vic Gabriel sensed the threat of danger in the air. He knew they were being watched, perhaps their every step across the platform was being monitored. Removing the protective goggles from his eyes, he lifted the Zeiss binoculars to his face. He searched the ridgeline to his immediate right, then raked the terrain beyond Attila's so-called Expedition Force Leviathan. There was a series of crevasses that flanked the ice face, about a hundred yards ahead. They would have to ascend those crevasses, he knew, to get a toehold on the ice face of Makalu from some ledge higher up. But whatever was at the top of those crevasses, Gabriel couldn't tell for certain.

The low cloud ceiling was perfect—for the Russians. Ambush weather, yeah. It was just too damn quiet for Gabriel's liking.

Standing, tugging the Dragunov sniper rifle higher up

on his shoulder, his ice ax hanging low on his leg from a thong, Gabriel set off after the expedition force.

Captain Blackwell was moving down the ledge when he heard the sound. He was just about to hammer another piton into ice....

Chopper!

Or was he hallucinating? Surely, his ordeal had pushed him to the edge of insanity. Twice he had attempted to fill his belly with the flesh of the dead. Twice he had vomited, nearly collapsed from nausea and repulsion. Finally, his stomach still empty, he had rigged the rappel rope, lowered himself down the steep, near-vertical face—perhaps all of four or five hundred feet. Body rappeling, he believed the alpiners called it. Hell, he didn't really know that much about mountaineering, but he was a master of logic. There were logical moves to anything. See the problem. Plan and evaluate. Attack the problem. At least the dead had left him with the essential equipment to attempt a descent.

But he was far from home free, he knew.

The driving wind now threatened to hurl him off the face of the Leviathan.

The mist and the snow whipped around the ledge, stinging Blackwell's face like angry hornets. Peering through his goggles, Blackwell searched the clouds that hugged the face of the mountain. He couldn't believe his ears and joked to himself that the mountain gods were just fucking around with him

But the sound came at him, carried to his ears, it seemed, on the whiplashing winds.

The whapping bleat grew into a steady throb. No, it can't be, he told himself. In this weather? At this altitude? Perhaps he was a lot farther down the mountain than he had originally believed. Choppers couldn't climb...

Then he saw the chopper, parting the mist, rising through the cloud bank below him. Moments later the chopper was hovering over the ledge, a great white bleating insect. Rotor wash pounded over Blackwell, spewing a cyclone of snow that blinded him for long moments.

The chopper was a blurry shadow behind the swirling snow. Any closer and there was a good chance, Blackwell knew, that a sudden gust of wind could slam the chopper into the mountain. Those fly-boys were taking a real chance, he thought. Elated, he thought about kissing each one of them full on the lips for their courageous effort. A night on the town, damn right, on him. Food. Drink. God! He was going to see his family again.

He was going home.

The rope ladder dropped in front of Blackwell. Caught in the furious rotor wash and driving winds, the ladder whipped, back and forth, at Blackwell. His only thought was rescue.

He was being saved from certain death.

Leaving himself tied to the rappel rope, Blackwell grabbed the ladder. Hope surged new life through his starved body.

Almost frantically, feeling a strange whimpering sound damning up in his throat, he climbed the ladder. Head down, he reached the fuselage doorway.

"Thank God! Thank God!" he said, his voice sounding far away in his ears, dreamlike in the hammering rotor wash.

Blackwell felt hands claw into his windsuit, haul him into the fuselage.

He knelt for a second, shaking uncontrollably. He felt the tears of relief squeeze into the corners of his eyes, a burning sensation, but one that made him feel alive, more alive than he could ever remember feeling in all of his life. Facing death had given him a new perspective on life. He felt like a new man, clean, pure. Wanting to laugh out loud and curse the mountain gods, he untied the rope from around his midsection, let it fall out the door and hurl itself back at Makalu.

He was alive.

He was saved.

Makalu be damned! He'd won. By God, he'd won!

And he had the Sphinx black box in the dead man's rucksack. The mission would be a success, after all.

Blackwell lifted his head. "Thank..."

Captain Blackwell felt the words strangle in his throat. He found himself staring right into the muzzle of an AK-47. Then he saw the red star on the breast of the Russian's whitesuit.

The Russian grinned down at Captain Blackwell.

Captain Blackwell felt his heart drop into his stomach.

The grin melted off the lips of Lieutenant Vorshilokov. "You were expecting someone else, comrade?"

Perched on the ledge, untying himself from the umbilical line, Lieutenant General Mikhail Vishtka had just received the news from his radio operator, Vladimir Okshoskya. It was incredible! Comrade Vorshilokov had plucked the Amerikanski spy pilot off the face of the mountain. And they had recovered the voice-and-film box that had recorded the spy pilot's criminal mission. The prize catch, *da. Nyet*, two prize catches. He could return to Moskva in triumph. The whole world would now see just what treachery, what barbaric acts the Amerikanskis were capable of.

But Vishtka was now faced with another problem. Their ascent now seemed pointless. Now they would have to go back down. He looked at the Mongol porters as they spread out across the ledge with the supplies. They would no longer be needed. They were now not only mouths to feed, but dead weight. He decided that he must kill them all and throw them down into the valley glacier before descending.

A second later, Vishtka found himself faced with another problem. A deadly problem.

Crouched in a pocket carved into the face of the ice wall by eons of vicious winds, Viktor Odeltmir lowered the field glasses, pointed toward the crevasse below. "Comrade Lieutenant General! Look!"

Removing his protective goggles, Vishtka grabbed the binoculars from Odeltmir. He adjusted the focus, peered through the high-powered infrared Stalin field glasses. And he saw the hunters as they appeared in a sudden wide break in the mist. They were roped together, inching their way up the crevasse, some five hundred feet below.

Vishtka lowered the Stalin field glasses. "Comrade Okshoskya!" he snapped at his radio operator. "Tell Lieutenant Vorshilokov to return to base camp with the prisoner immediately. Alert our motherships three and four to the situation. They are to lift off and close in immediately. Seal them off in the crevasse. They know what to do. Sergeant Jenenkov is in position there, and the attack will begin . . ." he said, suddenly talking to himself, "within minutes."

The hunters, Lieutenant General Mikhail Vishtka thought, were about to become the hunted.

Hunted dead.

Spindrift hissed down the crevasse, lashing at the expedition force. Working the slope second behind Attila, Vic Gabriel knew it would only be another hundred feet up the steep incline before they began hammering pitons that would earmark their assault against the ice face.

Gabriel heard Zac Dillinger and Johnny Simms grunting behind him. Simms and the ex-P.I. were struggling up the incline, cursing as they hacked at the ice with picks, digging crampons into the treacherous footing. Mountaineers they weren't, Gabriel decided. Cursing, hacking, expending valuable energy.

"Easy, easy back there," Gabriel said. "Want some advice?"

"Sure, why not?" Dillinger said gruffly. "You're gonna give it to me anyway."

"Relax," Gabriel said. "Like anything else, it's all attitude. You've gotta want to be here, *believe* you should be here on this rock. The higher up we get, the harder it's going to be. Keep your confidence. You start questioning why the hell you're here . . . that's when you fall."

"It ain't lack of confidence that's killing me, Vic," Johnny Simms said, his words hurled away by the wind that seemed funneled down the crevasse. "It's the goddamn cold!"

"What's that?"

Gabriel looked up at Attila, saw the operative searching the cloud bank above and to the left, peering intently through the slanting snowfall. And Gabriel heard it then, too.

"What's what?" Dillinger growled.

"That's what," Gabriel replied a second later.

Sweeping out of the clouds, the Mi-24 gunship swooped toward the crevasse.

Gabriel unslung his HK33, waiting for the 12.7mm gun to open up on them as the warbird swung into position to cut loose with lethal lead.

The MM1 was in Dillinger's hands.

Boolewarke, snatching the M60 and cartridge belt from his porter, raised the feed cover to belt the maneater.

The gunship soared past Gabriel. Rotor wash kicked up a cyclone of snow over the crevasse.

As the Mi-24 hovered for a second, Gabriel saw two men standing in the fuselage doorway. A Russian in whitesuit. That Russian had the muzzle of his AK-47 pressed into the neck of another man.

"God damn!" Attila yelled. "That's Blackwell!"

As if he'd heard and understood Attila's anger and disbelief, the Russian smiled down at the CIA operative.

Attila twisted around. Gabriel heard the operative shout down at the porters in Nepali, then told Eagle Force, "Hold your fire!"

Suddenly, Gabriel felt the line tugging at him. Someone had slipped. He turned, saw Dillinger struggling to haul himself out of the snow.

Then Gabriel checked on the porters in the rear.

The gunship swept down the crevasse, heading for the valley glacier. Watching the warbird fly on, Gabriel then spotted movement from below.

From behind the porters in the rear.

Figures were springing up out of the snow in pockets on both sides of the crevasse.

Whitesuited figures with automatic weapons.

Before he could shout a warning, AK-47s were blazing, slugs stitching into the porters.

Screams ripped up the crevasse.

Chapter 13

Autofire roared.

The weight of dead Sherpas pulled Eagle Force down the crevasse.

"Cut the line!" Gabriel shouted at his commandos, unsheathing his Ka-Bar and slicing through rope with one savage swipe.

Dillinger fell away from Gabriel, cursing, the ex-P.I.'s Ka-Bar streaking for rope.

Johnny Simms struggled to unsling his HK33, but rope twisted around his shoulders, pinning him to the floor of the crevasse as he hit the snow. Slugs sliced into the ice wall beside the black ex-merc.

Below Gabriel, the line of tracking lead was rapidly chewing up the line of porters. Sherpas twisted, great hunks of fur and blood splashing over the walls of the crevasse as 7.62mm ComBloc lead hornets swarmed over them.

The advantage of surprise on their side, the Russian executioners held their ground, automatic weapons bucking, flaming in their hands.

Slicing themselves free from the umbilical line, Eagle Force galvanized into action. Gabriel threw himself against the wall of the crevasse as lead bit into the snow beside him. As the din of autofire hurled up the crevasse at them, Eagle Force unleashed a furious return barrage at the SPETSNAZ Red Star commandos.

HK33 chattering on full auto, Gabriel churned up a whitesuited figure with a 3-round burst of .223 Remington lead.

Throwing his commando dagger aside, Boolewarke flung himself sideways, the Dutchman hugging the crevasse's wall, shoulders sinking into snow. M60 roaring, he hosed down six Russians, kicking them back down the crevasse, blood spurting from the ragged holes in their whitesuits. Blood that froze seconds after spattering the snow.

Above, Gabriel heard the bark of Attila's M-16 as the operative opened up to join the slaughter.

Or be slaughtered.

Lead burned down the crevasse.

Fumbling to unsling AK-47s from their shoulders, still roped together, Sherpas cried out. Before the Sherpas had a chance to return fire, ComBloc lead tore into them, flinging them into each other behind jetting crimson washes. A chunk of *Sirdar* Amaka's head puked off as the lead hellstorm pealed over him.

A slug bit through the rope binding *Ang* Bhantaj to his dead and dying brothers. He dashed out of the crossfire hurricane of bullets like a wink of lightning. Unflinching in the blazing eye of lead, slugs peppering the snow around him, the young Sherpa loaded his bow, loosed the arrow. Downrange, Sergeant Jenenkov grabbed at his face, blood streaming from his eye where the arrowhead had drilled him into a half-blind man and pierced his brain. Jenenkov toppled as lead ripped his whitesuit to scarlet rags.

On their backs, Johnny Simms and Zac Dillinger directed relentless HK33 autofire at Russians already spinning death pirouettes. Bullet-riddled Marxist corpses tumbled down the crevasse, flopping head-over-heels in a trail of crimson gore.

"Bloody Buddha!" Boolewarke shouted over the deafening stutter of autofire. Then a slug ripped across the

Dutchman's shoulder. Wincing, he glanced at his shoulder. Blood wealed through the whitesuit where the bald eagle emblem had been. Howling in some berserker rage, Boolewarke, slugs twirling around his face, raked the Russians with merciless sprays of 7.62mm NATO lead.

"Vic! Look!" Dillinger shouted, pointing skyward. "Just what we need! More trouble!"

Gabriel spotted the white-camoued Mi-24 as it surged out of the mist, banking in from the ice face. Angling away from the crevasse, the predatory gunship streaked toward the mouth of the fissure—a gravesite bloated with falling bodies. Just then Gabriel, slapping home a fresh 30-round clip in the HK33, saw another Mi-24 heading for the killing zone. That warbird seemed to swoop from straight out of the sky. Hugging the face of Makalu dangerously close from almost a thousand feet above the crevasse, the gunship hovered all of a sudden.

To launch a few rockets, Gabriel knew, *and send us all for a ride up the face of the Leviathan.*

Attila reacted to the threat instantly. Hefting the M-16, he sighted down on the gunship.

Bad Zac Dillinger pulled the MM1 off his shoulder.

They were hemmed in, Gabriel knew, and both warbirds were about to chew them up into Nepali cheese.

Then Johnny Simms scooped up two discarded RPG-7s, both armed with warheads.

"Vic!" he yelled, and tossed Gabriel one of the rocket launchers.

The gunship hovering over the valley glacier cut loose with 12.7mm minigun fire. A line of slugs marched up the crevasse, exploding puffs of snow over the dead.

More Sherpas died as the rain of lead drilled them into the snow.

Ang Bhantaj nose-dived into a pocket, slugs thudding into the bodies of his dead brothers.

The gunship blazed fire and lead into the crevasse.

Zac Dillinger, teeth gritted, triggered his MM1.

A 40mm hellbomb chugged from Attila's M203.

Round after 38mm round belched from Dillinger's MM1, the projectiles streaking toward the Mi-24 suspended over the mouth of the crevasse.

Wind tore down the crevasse. Snow swirled around Eagle Force as lead drilled into the ice walls.

Minigun fire pulped a Sherpa into a blood-bursting sack.

Together, Gabriel and Simms triggered their RPGs as Attila's warhead shot past the warbird and pounded into the face of Makalu.

A huge snow cloud vomited off the Leviathan.

A gigantic ball of fire flashed over the mouth of the crevasse.

Gabriel held his breath, knowing the gunship was just within the effective 300-meter range of the RPG-7. A split second later, both 85mm warheads struck.

True and lethal.

Hulks of twisted wreckage spewed from the boiling firecloud, suspended for a moment, it seemed, by gale-force winds. Behind Gabriel, Simms watched as the sky lit up in an orange-red blaze.

Fire in the wind.

Flaming debris slammed off the mountain, then plummeted for the razorback ridgeline beyond the crevasse.

Vic Gabriel, the RPG-7 lowering by his side, listened to the wind and the crackling fire.

Then he heard the rumble.

Lieutenant General Mikhail Vishtka heard the rumble, too. Terror gripped his heart as the wreckage spun off the mountain, sheets of debris plunging from out of the roiling flames, falling, then pounding off the ledge. A piece of wreckage clipped Vladimir Okshoskya, kicked him off the ledge, the radio backpack crushed under a jagged piece of rotor blade.

Vishtka heard Okshoskya's scream, but those chilling screams were drowned out a second later by an even more ominous sound.

A sound like thunder that Vishtka heard pealing directly overhead. The SPETSNAZ lieutenant general felt the ledge quaking beneath him.

A wave of snow hammered over the Russians and their porters.

But Vishtka knew the real hammering had only begun.

In a panic, the Sherpa porters charged their Russian captors. Flaming AK-47s mowed six Sherpas down, hurling them off the ledge and sending them plunging for the valley glacier. Obviously realizing it was suicide to attempt to overpower the heavily armed Russians, the Sherpas hugged the face of the mountain, bracing themselves for the worst.

Vishtka knew there was only one chance to escape the avalanche. He believed he could prevent being buried alive beneath acres of snow if he hugged the wall, deep inside the pocket. It would be like crawling, a whipped dog, away from danger, cowering in a corner while the threat passed. A despicable image of himself, he thought. But there was no alternative. He cursed the enemy but realized his gunship pilot had kept the Mi-24 too close to the mountain while lining up to launch the 57mm warheads. Now Vishtka was about to pay the price for the pilot's fatal miscalculation. Not only had the Mi-24 been blown out of the sky, but its wreckage had caused the avalanche.

Vishtka looked up, just as the wall of snow sloughed off the face of the Leviathan.

It sounded as if the sky had split asunder. It felt as if the earth were breaking open to swallow them whole.

Giant manna from heaven, Vic Gabriel thought as he looked up the slope and watched for two heartbeats as acres of snow slid down the face of Makalu, rumbling in a full-pitched fury. Hell from heaven.

The ex-CIA assassin knew he had less than a few seconds to act.

The Russian bastards on the ledge were slaughtering the Sherpas like sheep and hurling them down into the valley. In their brutal attempt to make more room for themselves on the ledge, Gabriel saw the Russians open up with blazing AK-47 autofire. Three more Sherpas were launched away from the ledge, arms windmilling as they plunged for the valley glacier, hundreds of feet below.

"What are you doing, Vic?" Zac Dillinger yelled, the rumble of the avalanche pounding through the crevasse.

"We've gotta get the hell down the crevasse! We'll be buried alive!" Johnny Simms shouted.

"Too late for that," Gabriel answered, feeling the wall and floor of the crevasse trembling violently around him. "Hug the wall and hope most of the snow slides down the lip of the crevasse. And pray the mountain gods have a sense of justice!"

"Mountain gods! Bloody Kali's fuck!" Boolewarke roared. "Sounds like you've spent too much time in Nepal already."

Gabriel was grimly intent on payback. Russian payback. Hefting the 7.62mm SVD sniper rifle, sighting through the PSO-1 scope, he fixed grim deathsights on the Russian scrambling for cover in the pocket. Beside him, Gabriel heard frantic yelling.

"What's the matter with him?" Johnny Simms, glancing at Karzim Bhantaj, asked Attila.

"He says he saw his old man up there!"

The rumble grew louder as the tidal wave of snow began to thunder, a white tongue as long as a football field, pounding Makalu.

148

For just a brief second, Gabriel lined up a Russian face of fear in the crosshairs.

A heartbeat was all he needed.

Vic Gabriel squeezed the trigger.

The Dragunov bucked in Gabriel's fists.

It was going to be Lieutenant General Mikhail Vishtka's final act of vengeance. *This one's for his ancestors,* he thought, pivoting and swinging the AK-47 toward the old kahn. His finger tightening around the trigger, Vishtka was rooted to the spot near the lip of the ledge. He looked Timur Bhantaj dead in the eye. He wanted to smile, to savor the moment, but there was no time.

The avalanche was roaring, less than a hundred meters above.

Then the back of Vishtka's head exploded in a podburst of blood, brains, and ragged strips of whitesuit. The 7.62mm slug, muzzling at 830 meters per second, kicked Vishtka into the pocket.

Timur Bhantaj moved for the pocket, then froze as Viktor Odeltmir turned the AK-47 on him. The AK-47 chattered, but the line of slugs ripped into the ice face above Bhantaj.

Viktor Odeltmir slammed, facedown, into the pocket, the AK-47 spinning away from the ledge.

But Timur Bhantaj saw that Viktor Odeltmir had no face. Indeed, Viktor Odeltmir had no head left above the gleaming shards of jawbone.

Several Russians and the surviving Sherpas scrambled into the pocket.

The main tongue of the avalanche descended over the ledge.

A heartbeat after his second sniping kill, Vic Gabriel hit the floor of the crevasse.

Paralyzed with fear, Eagle Force hugged the wall of

the fissure. Gabriel could almost feel each man there holding his breath.

Grim anticipation.

Death descent.

The earth trembled.

The sky roared.

A great tidal wave of snow hammered over the lip of the crevasse.

Eagle Force braced themselves as the snow swept over the crevasse, slamming off the lip.

Chapter 14

The mountain gods had smiled down on them, all right, Vic Gabriel thought, and thanked his lucky stars. Shaking the snow off his HK33, he found himself buried, waist-deep, in a snow mound. But they were alive, and that was all that mattered. *Nature does work in mysterious ways,* he thought. *Hell, maybe there really is some unseen force that guides the hands of certain men. Maybe my father. . . .*

There was a hollow silence in the air, a silence that seemed to carry weight to Vic Gabriel. A weight that fell square on his shoulders. Wounded, dead weight on his conscience, right. The Sherpa dead.

Then the wind moaned, a somber requiem for the dead.

Attila, then Simms, Boolewarke, and Dillinger stood.

"That was quick," Johnny Simms said, exhaling a pent-up breath.

"And damn lucky," Boolewarke growled, his M60 almost untouched by snow.

For some reason, the main tongue of the avalanche had skirted the lip of the crevasse, bypassing the fissure for the most part and surging on into the valley. Even still, snow had piled ten feet high along the north lip.

"Maybe there are mountain gods, after all," Henry van Boolewarke said.

"And maybe more Russians," Attila pointed out, brushing

the snow off his hood and whitesuit. "Like down in the valley."

Which presented another problem for Eagle Force. Captain Blackwell and the Sphinx black box.

"Where's young Bhantaj?" Gabriel said, worried, looking down the crevasse. Farther down, the snow had piled higher, almost blocking the way out of the fissure. Beyond the snow wall stretched the platform.

The valley glacier of death.

The final killing field.

Simms and Boolewarke, fighting through the snow, dug through the closest mounds with their hands, kicking savagely at the snow with their feet. Simms pulled up the arm of a dead Sherpa, saw that it wasn't young Bhantaj.

Moments later, a head poked out of a snow mound.

Vic Gabriel and Zac Dillinger pulled *Ang* Bhantaj out of the snow. Because of the snow piled along the lip of the crevasse, there was no way to see the ledge above and beyond. No telling if there were any survivors in that pocket on the ledge.

Gabriel suspected that the men on that ledge had either been kicked down into the valley or were now buried alive. It became obvious to Gabriel that Karzim Bhantaj suspected this, too. Anger flashed through the young Sherpa's dark eyes, then he seemed to wilt with despair. He said something in his native tongue. A chant, Gabriel believed.

"What did he say?" Gabriel asked Attila.

"A prayer for his father's soul."

"Goddamned Ivans," Henry van Boolewarke rasped.

There were six Russians in the fuselage of the Mi-24. Captain Blackwell weighed his odds, decided they weren't good.

But he was going for broke.

The Sphinx black box was sitting on the floorboard,

the grand prize for the Russians to take back to Moscow. And his capture, he knew, would fan the flames of suspicion and distrust between East and West. The cold war would turn hot, soon, very soon. No way in hell was he going to be paraded before the world as a criminal acting on orders from his own country in a treacherous attack against the Russian satellite compound.

No way in goddamn hell.

Lies on top of lies. That was all the Russians knew. Lies.

Three of the bastards, Blackwell saw, had their backs turned to him. They were looking out across the platform, searching for the men, he assumed, who had been in the crevasse.

Americans. CIA? Blackwell wondered. If the avalanche had pounded over them in that fissure, Blackwell knew he'd never discover their identity.

Perhaps it didn't really matter, he decided. He had been on his own since bailing out of *Lightning Bolt*.

It was time to act. Time to stare Death in the face again. And spit in Death's eye.

His nerves were frayed, his adrenaline racing. Two Russians near the cockpit door. One Ivan beside him. All of them armed with AK-47s.

Captain Blackwell decided he had no choice. He had already been pronounced guilty by Little Mother Russia. But he wasn't DOA. Not yet.

Blackwell lunged at the Russian beside him. With a knife-edged hand, he crushed that Russian's windpipe. As Blackwell snatched the AK-47 out of the gagging Russian's hands, Lieutenant Vorshilokov and the two Russians flanking him spun.

Blackwell triggered the AK-47, stitching a line of slugs across the chest of Vorshilokov.

But the two Russians near the cockpit door reacted to the threat with lightning speed.

Screaming in a berserker rage, Blackwell charged the Russians beside the tumbling corpse of Vorshilokov, sweeping a long spray over them.

Then a stream of 7.62mm ComBloc lead tore into Blackwell. The captain felt the fire, searing every nerve end in his body. He wheeled, directing autofire at the Russians near the cockpit.

Another Russian tumbled to the floorboard, his blood spraying over the fuselage.

Slugs ripped open Blackwell's windsuit.

It had been a stupid thing to do, Blackwell heard a voice in the back of his head chide him in his dying moment.

The mission was a wash.

ComBloc lead shredded Captain Blackwell's windsuit, kicked him out the door.

There was no choice. Attila had told Vic Gabriel he wanted that gunship whole, not blown off the platform. There was a good chance the Sphinx black box had been recovered with the capture of Captain Blackwell.

But Captain Blackwell was dead. Seconds ago, Gabriel had seen Blackwell reeling out the fuselage door. Shot to hell.

Trudging desperately through the snow, their weapons spitting lead at the gunship, Gabriel and Attila spread out. From the snow mounds piled in the mouth of the crevasse, Simms, Boolewarke, and Dillinger hammered the fuselage doorway with a relentless hail of lead.

Under the blanket of covering fire, Gabriel and Attila closed on the gunship. One lone Russian, Gabriel saw, was the last survivor on the killing field. One lone Russian stood between them and . . . and what? Gabriel wondered. Success? If the Sphinx black box wasn't there, then just what the hell had they come to Nepal for? To take a Russian body count?

Just moments ago, Blackwell had gone berserk, but Gabriel knew the guy had been through one helluva nightmarish ordeal. He'd broken down and rolled the dice.

Crapped out.

Boolewarke's M60 roared as he raked the gunship's hull with a hurricane of NATO lead. HK33s stuttering, Dillinger and Simms expended clip after clip, keeping the Russian in the doorway pinned down, not allowing him a chance to open fire on Gabriel and Attila as they charged across the stretch of no-man's-land.

Gabriel and Attila flung themselves against the hull of the Mi-24. With a wave of his hand, the commandos ceased fire.

Silence.

For a second, Vic Gabriel looked down at the bullet-churned corpse of Captain Blackwell. He didn't know a damn thing about Blackwell, except the guy was a high-flying spy cowboy for the CIA. He'd done his job for the Company, but in the process he'd gotten burned. Faced with a humiliating incarceration by the Russians, the guy had made his choice. Fight instead of being imprisoned and used by the Russians as a media event. Gabriel gave the guy credit for guts. Even though he was dead, perhaps Blackwell had made the right choice. The only choice.

The wind soughed over the platform.

Gabriel and Attila began inching their way down the hull, closing on the fuselage door.

The muzzle of an AK-47 poked through the doorway.

A sharp cry ripped the air beside Gabriel.

At almost the same instant, Gabriel and Attila converged on the doorway. A pencil-tip of flame stabbed at Gabriel. Lead spanged off the doorway as Gabriel ducked, feeling the lead nicking his hood and biting off a chunk of cloth. Whirling into the doorway, Gabriel cut loose on the Russian, his HK33 stammering on full-auto slaughter.

Attila's M-16 flamed.

Twin streams of lead drove the Russian across the fuselage, pinned him to the wall. Blood gushed from gaping wounds in his whitesuit. He jerked, twitched, then finally bounced off the wall and slammed to the floor-board. As he hit the floor, the arrowshaft snapped in half. Young Bhantaj, Gabriel saw, had drilled the Russian in the upper arm. Had perhaps saved his life when the Russian was about to make his move.

Gabriel checked the fuselage. He took a body count as Attila jumped into the fuselage moving toward the cockpit. Moments later, satisfied that the last of the Russian SPETSNAZ commandos had been killed, Gabriel turned, slumped against the hull. He was tired. Dead on his feet.

The three commandos and Bhantaj, bow in hand, high-stepped through the deep snow.

"That it?" Boolewarke called out, his voice echoing across the platform.

Gabriel nodded. "All dead and accounted for. Attila, tell Bhantaj he did good," the ex-CIA assassin said. Twisting his head, he found Attila standing right beside him.

Attila held the Sphinx black box in his hand. Gabriel glimpsed the triumphant smile on the guy's lips and stifled the urge to yank him out of the gunship and kick the shit out of him. How many had died to recover that damn box? How many lives could've been spared if the son of a bitch had listened to him and just left behind the Sherpas?

"That's what all the fuss was about?" Zac Dillinger said gruffly, closing down on the gunship.

"You bet," Attila said, jumping out of the doorway, landing with catlike grace in the snow. He looked at the Sphinx black box for a moment. "Ain't it beautiful. Now we can go home, soldier."

"Can you fly this bird?" Gabriel asked Attila.

"Nope. Guess we hike it back."

"One lousy mission recorder," Boolewarke said, shaking his head, a note of sorrow and anger in his voice. "And all these dead men. Just to keep the cold war from turning hot. Christ."

"It doesn't seem right, does it, Vic?" Dillinger said.

Gabriel looked at Zac Dillinger. He didn't say a word. No, it didn't seem right. Not one goddamn bit.

Vic Gabriel heard Makalu speak for him.

The Leviathan rumbled.

Well into the next morning, they reached Tamerlane. Wreckage had burned out, white lumps now beneath a fresh carpet of snow. Harsh sunlight glared off the snow-capped peaks of the Himalayas.

Gabriel, HK33 slung around his shoulder, led Eagle Force toward the armored jeep. In silence, they had trudged down the trail and into Tamerlane, fighting off the bitter cold, knowing that they were going home. It had been a long night.

The villagers moved out of their yurts, walked up to young Bhantaj.

Suddenly Gabriel heard the commotion. He turned, saw a figure stepping off the trail.

"Well, how about that?" Attila, walking up behind Eagle Force, said. "The khan's returned. He must be one tough old son of a bitch."

Gabriel watched as father and son were reunited.

"How in the hell?" Attila wondered aloud.

Gabriel didn't know. Most likely, the khan had dug himself out of the snow on the ledge, rappeled himself down the mountain.

Timur Bhantaj was the only Sherpa, besides his son, who had walked out of the valley of death. Gabriel was happy for father and son. He wished that . . .

Then something happened. Something that Vic Gabriel had suspected would happen all along. As father and son embraced, Attila drew down on Eagle Force with his M-16.

"Well, look at this guy," Zac Dillinger rasped.

"Don't turn around," Attila warned.

Eagle Force froze.

"Is that what you call a BA, Hun honey?" Dillinger spat.

"I call it finishing unfinished business," Attila began. "You see, you comedians were never meant to make a curtain call."

"We had 'em pegged right, huh, Victor?" the Dutchman said.

"But you didn't act on your gut feelings. Too bad for you," Attila said, and an ugly grin stretched his lips. "I'm not sure exactly why SOD wants you terminated, but hey, I've got my orders. What can I tell ya? Hey, I'm sorry. No hard feelings, huh?"

"Why did you even bother?" Gabriel asked.

"What bother? You soldiers were a tremendous help in mopping up on Ivan. You've outlived your usefulness, though. Maybe the whole deal was to get you here and leave you here, I don't know, and I don't really care. I'm tired, hungry, and want to get home."

"Did you ever think that maybe SOD's got some guns waiting for you Stateside, Attila?" Gabriel posed.

Attila hesitated for a moment, and Gabriel could sense the wheels spinning in his head.

"Not if I've got the Sphinx, they don't. I know how to deal with them. I can—"

The arrowhead speared into Attila's shoulder.

Eagle Force saw their chance, took lightning, deadly advantage of their opening. Spinning in unison, they unleashed a wall of lead on Attila. Attila's M-16 barked a 3-round burst skyward.

Boolewarke's M60 roared. HK33s stammering on full-auto, Gabriel, Simms, and Dillinger pounded Attila into the snow, chopping his whitesuit up into bloody shreds.

When their guns fell silent, Gabriel stared down at the leaking corpse.

"Now that's what I call an acceptance of an apology," Zac Dillinger said.

"No hard feelings, Attila, right," Vic Gabriel said.

The ex-CIA assassin turned, looked at *Ang* Bhantaj. The bow lowered by the young Sherpa's side. Gabriel wanted to thank the Sherpa, but he didn't know any Nepali.

Even still, Gabriel knew his eyes spoke for him.

Young Bhantaj showed Eagle Force a fleeting smile.

Torquemada laid the phone down gently. He wanted to scream, tear the walls to the beachfront condominium down in a fit of rage. He held his fury in check, looked at Sprenger. Anger would be wasted energy at this point.

"It looks as if the dogs have returned to their own vomit," Torquemada said.

"And our operatives?"

"Dead. Gabriel has the Sphinx. He wants us to meet him at the so-called Gator Base Burning Bush."

"Call in the cleanup crew?"

"Yeah. The dogs are about to eat their own vomit."

Epilogue

The four airboats slid up to the pier.

Sunset burned, a flaming crimson wash, over the Everglades.

Sprenger and Torquemada, Uzi submachine guns in hand, disembarked from the airboats. Torquemada ran down the pier, heading toward the command HQ.

From the mangrove treeline beyond the obstacle course, Eagle Force watched as the dozen hitters spread out on the pier.

Those hitters were armed to the teeth. Those hitters were marked for a hellstorm, Vic Gabriel knew.

Gabriel and Dillinger, crouched beside an XM-174 automatic grenade launcher, waited. M-16s were slung around the shoulders of the four commandos. Beads of sweat trickled down over the granite-hard expressions of Simms and Boolewarke. Simms fisted the sweat out of his eyes.

"Wait, wait," Gabriel breathed, listening to the feet pounding over the rickety wood of the pier. He gripped the hellbox, knowing he was talking more to himself than his commandos.

It was all going to end here. Or was it? Gabriel wondered. For damn sure they were going to have to move their base of operations. Probably overseas. Either way, he knew the Company wasn't just about to close their eyes to this ugly little affair.

Behind Eagle Force rested the weapons bins and other essentials they had cleared out of the command HQ.

Torquemada hit a combat crouch beside the open doorway to the command HQ, fanning the interior with his Uzi. The command post was empty.

Then Torquemada saw the Sphinx black box. It sat in the doorway of the empty HQ. Right in front of him.

"It's here. I've found it," he called out to Sprenger. "Move 'em out and search the—"

Gabriel pressed the button.

And the command HQ was vaporized, hurled skyward in sawtooth shards on a roaring mountain of fire.

The Company hitters belly flopped on the pier as jagged shards of wood and tongues of fire blew over them.

The XM-174 chugged out a stream of 40mm grenades. Eagle Force unslung their M-16s, triggering their assault rifles on full-auto and spewing more confusion and chaos into the target zone.

And hurling death.

Sprenger was up and running across the field before the first line of explosions raked the pier. Suddenly, as bodies cartwheeled through the smoke and flames behind him, Sprenger pitched to the soft earth, screaming. He grabbed at his mangled leg. Horrified, he saw that the razor-sharp teeth of the bear trap had nearly bitten his lower leg clean in half. Jagged shinbone jutted out of the spurting blood. Wild-eyed, face twisted in agony, he searched for his M-16. The assault rifle had flown from his grasp, lay three feet in front of him. Sprenger gagged on his own vomit.

The airboats were pulverized by the 40mm grenade barrage. Twisted metal spun through the air. Bits and pieces of wet meat spattered the water around the airboats being rapidly chopped up into scrap.

A searing fireball whooshed down the pier, puking up

planks and incinerating assassins, silencing their screams forever.

Gabriel and Eagle Force stood. M-16s trained on Sprenger, who thrashed around on the soft earth, Eagle Force slowly headed toward the Company operative.

"Not a bad idea, laying all those bear traps, Victor," the Dutchman congratulated.

"Except we snared a rat," Dillinger growled.

Sprenger crabbed across the ground. He reached for his M-16, wrapped his hand around the assault rifle.

A combat boot stomped down on Sprenger's hand, pinning the M-16 to the earth.

Terror carved Sprenger's face. Greasy bile dripping off his chin, Sprenger stared up at Vic Gabriel.

Gabriel flicked the mode on his M-16 for a 3-round burst.

"The mission was a wash, friend Sprenger," Gabriel said, grim, tight-lipped. "And you're washed up. I don't even want to know the why."

Gabriel pumped a 3-round burst into Sprenger's face.

Wreckage drifted for the swampland.

Fire crackled along the smoking pier.

"Now what?" Johnny Simms wondered aloud.

"We move, that's what," Vic Gabriel answered.

"To where?" Zac Dillinger wanted to know. "They'll come after us again. Maybe not today. Maybe not tomorrow. But sometime, you can bet our Swiss bank accounts on it, the Company will be back."

"Don't bet our Swiss stash, Bad One, please," Simms said. "I got a week in Atlantic City lined up for us."

"No titty bars this time, you wildass dumbfucks," Henry van Boolewarke growled.

"So what are we supposed to do now? Move to where, VG?" Dillinger asked.

"I don't know," Gabriel growled. "We'll find some place. Hell, get out a map, close your eyes, and point."

"The way things are goin'," Johnny Simms said, "our fingers'll probably land on Nepal."

I hear ya, Johnny, I hear ya, Vic Gabriel thought, and stared into the flames crackling down the pier. *It's getting tougher by the day to be an independent. The way things are going, hell, we'll either be dead, in prison, or applying for welfare by the end of the month.*

KILLHUNT!

It's payback time for Eagle Force leader Vic Gabriel after two of his men are beaten and kidnapped by his longtime hated enemy, Mike Saunders. It's a ploy by the cunning Saunders to smoke out the ex-Delta Force commando—and trap him in a

RING
OF
FIRE

Here's an exciting preview of Book #5 in Dan Schmidt's EAGLE FORCE series:

RING
OF
FIRE

EAGLE FORCE: *They're coming at you!*

Look for EAGLE FORCE wherever Bantam Books are sold.

1

There were two of them, and they were dead men. Two for now, he decided, and the other two later. They were dead already, though, in a very real sense, the scar-faced man determined. *Only they didn't know it yet.* They were dead men walking, because they were soldiers, and real soldiers would never allow themselves to be trapped in the predicament those two were about to find themselves in. Dead meat. *Dead hanging meat* while buried in the warm wet flesh of some Parisian whores.

The tall scar-faced man stood in the deep shadows of the doorway. Lightning strobed, thunder cannoned. A torrential downpour hammered the cobblestone street, rain hissing off stone and brick like a thousand venomous serpents around him. Gray eyes peering off into the gray mist, he searched the alleyway across from him. Gaudy neon signs still flickered in the night, soliciting the denizens who would sell their souls for several dark hours of perversion. Shadows, he noted, still combed the crevices in the slitted lumpy blocks that grew out of the maze of streets like festering sores on the Left Bank, *Rive Gauche*, those dark souls searching to set free the twisted demons in themselves. They were mere germs in the light anyway, he decided, but they were something even more despicable, even more parasitic in the dark.

But wasn't Paris called the City of Light? the scar-faced man thought, and smiled a tight-lipped smile to himself. He touched his scar, felt a surge of contempt for all the students and artists and other demented minds that flooded the *grands boulevards* and *cafe-theatres* during the day. Day, though, had long since melted into night. And what manmade light brightened the night would soon be drowned by a wave of darkness, he told himself. Life would give way to death. Pleasure would scream into pain. And the mangled bodies would pile up on the conveyor belt of death.

He traced his scar with a long bony finger. It ran across the bridge of his nose, jagged down his cheek, and ended at his jawbone. The scar was war memorabilia, ill gotten recently in a time and a place the rest of the world had long since forgotten. He had done things that would make ordinary men cringe, vomit in horror. Indeed, he had done things that had made his own kind wince.

But he was proud. At least, *he* was a soldier.

Through the driving rain, he saw his man approach. Like himself, his man was dressed in black, and a long black leather trenchcoat concealed the armament he would use.

The shadow slid up to the scar-faced man.

"When, sir?" the shadow asked, his voice touched with a British accent.

Thunder boomed. Lightning ripped across the angry sky. Natural and unnatural light seemed to fuse for the briefest of seconds, far beyond the Left Bank. The scar-faced man thought he glimpsed the Eiffel Tower in the distance, nine-hundred and eighty-four feet of steel skeleton. Thought, because the night was full of shadows, and impending doom. Lightning seemed to be playing tricks on his eyes, and the peal of thunder was capable of drowning the loudest of noises at this hour of the morning.

Protected from the driving rain by an awning, the scar-faced man reached inside his trenchcoat. He pulled out a stainless steel Walther PPK/S, and screwed a silencer onto the deadly little pocket pistol.

"Our people ready?" He had no distinct accent, although he spoke at least a dozen languages fluently. He considered himself apart from the world, a cultureless entity unto himself.

The shadow kept his voice steady with respect. "We've been ready, sir. Two days we've been watching them. Two days and two nights now, we've watched them."

"They're softened up, soldier, good and soft now. Let's move in. Call it."

The shadow pulled a walkie-talkie from inside his trenchcoat.

As the scar-faced man stepped out into the hammering needlelike drops of rain he felt good. Damn good. He was strong. He was ready.

He had returned from the grave, he thought. He had been in exile too long.

It was payback time.

As he shadowed beneath the jagged fingers of lamplight and forged into the driving rain he turned his head in both directions. From opposite ends of the street, he saw them. Twenty-four dark shadows marched through the pounding downpour. Slowly, but in a kind of cadence, he noted.

Into the alley, the scar-faced man led those shadows. And they marched in cadence to the fierce crackle of lightning and the peal of thunder ripping from the black heavens.

Something warned him he shouldn't have been drinking, because when he drank he got drunk. And when Bad Zac Dillinger got drunk the world had better look out. Of course, experience had always dictated to the tall, granite-faced, white-haired ex-P.I. from sunny Fort Lauderdale that when he got drunk his world consisted of one thing, and usually one thing only. Whoring.

As he stared out the window and watched the rain hammer the dark alley and blocks of low-lying buildings across from him, he thought that there was an art to whoring. *You have to know when, how much and how long to let the whore in you run wild, then know when to bottle it up and walk away from it.* Right. Unfortunately he knew he didn't have the finer points of that art worked out, and certainly the rough edges of his lust would never be smoothed out. Kind of like his drinking, he determined. Once he started, he couldn't or didn't want to stop. It was a shame in a big way, he thought, that the two things he enjoyed most in life he was absolutely powerless to control. But there was always hope, wasn't there, that some day he'd find a way to get a handle on his vices and make them work to his advantage? Wasn't there?

No, there really wasn't, he knew. Hell, he had two ex-wives, golddigging sluts that would have shamed the most insatiable trollops out of Sodom and Gomorrah, that proved he had no control over what other people did. In a way, that knowledge alone was the only thing that kept him sane. Once a man can admit to himself he has no control, then he can begin to control the greatest single obstacle in his life. Himself. And in the end, Zac Dillinger thought, just what was he anyway? He was just a male version of what he dumped his lust into. He just happened to be a whore who could kick a whole lot of ass. And as for the female version of himself that he felt he so desperately needed? *A whore is a whore is a whore*, he thought, and felt a sadness hollow out the pit of his belly, *but God love 'em, because if He don't I sure will.*

And lovin' 'em all, he'd been doing. For two straight days and nights. Love or lust, it didn't really matter to him. They were both one and the same thing, weren't they? If they weren't, then it never really hurt a man to lie to himself a little in certain situations. *Lie to himself* if he could let it all go, walk away from the bottled-up genie when the time came. Unfortunately, Bad Zac Dillinger never got his fill and he never walked away from it, just pried himself free when the fear grew out of some mounting anxiety that warned him he would be trapped in his own little personal hell forever.

Two days and two nights of drinking and whoring. He then thought he should've been concerned about something else, too. *The silver bullet that's out there for every werewolf*: AIDS. Then, he shoved that grim thought out of his mind, told himself, *hell with it, it can only kill you once.*

Softly, he shook his head to himself, listening to the crackle of lightning and the peal of thunder that had clamped itself over the supposed City of Light, as if the ferocious downpour was some omen from Him. His mouth tasted like something nasty had popped up out of a toilet bowl and landed square in his throat, his head ached and swirled in nausea from about a few thousand francs worth of booze, and he didn't think he could get it up again if he used a shoe horn. But he wasn't finished, far from it. Drained for the moment, but not done, and the dark spirit of good unclean fun was sure to come roaring back any second. And therein, he knew, lay the insanity. He'd already paved the way with a heart of burning lust and a belly full of booze. And now the jaws of insanity were open wide to swallow him whole because he was standing at the end of a dead-end road. It was dark, and it was lonely there, but there was no turning back, simply because there was nothing to turn back to. Now he felt the fear. Cold and creeping, inching up his spine, ice worms squirming over the cracked pavement of his madness.

And the sorrow reached deeper into his guts.

What leads a man to this point in his life? he wondered. Where does it all begin? Where does it all end? The gray area, he believed, is where it all begins. Where it all ends is black-and-white. To even consider where it all might end was damn near terrifying in itself. Might? he scoffed to himself. Might nothing.

"Bay-bee, bay-bee, what is wrong? *Etendez-vous la, s'il vous plait.* Come lay down over here. Mee-chell will take good care of big bad white-haired man again. *S'il vous plait?*"

He peeked out the window, surveying the alley one more time. A couple of shadows in a doorway, a man and a woman. Nothing much seemed to be happening at this hour. But something was suddenly bugging the hell out of Zac Dillinger. He couldn't put a finger on it. He felt he shouldn't trust the night. Something was tugging at his guts, the same uneasy feeling he always got moments before danger reared itself in his face with foam flying and fangs glistening.

Turning, he glanced back at the whores. There were four of them. A brunette, a redhead, a dark-haired whore, and a big black one built like some Amazon queen. Red was patting the sheets, imploring him with her green cat eyes to come back to bed. Dillinger looked at Johnny Simms. The black ex-merc was shucking himself into his pants. As he delved into his pants pocket, a concerned expression froze on the black ex-merc's face. Then, standing there in white boxer shorts, sporting all the countless scars from old knife and bullet wounds all over his back and torso, Bad Zac let his gaze wander back over the four lovelies. They were looking at those old wounds. He knew he must look like some kind of freak show to them, but there was a glint in their eyes that told him they found his roughhewn, scarred old warhorse's carcass desirable. Women never did make much sense to him. And French women, he had discovered, weren't exactly wholesome and glowing with virtue, and they certainly weren't what he would call beautiful. They seemed to be painted just right, though, and carry just the right amount of arrogance that made them all appeal to the animal in the male of the species. The four whores were sipping wine and champagne out of little crystal goblets. Dillinger fixed a long second's stare on hardened nipples that showed just over the edge of red satin sheets. They giggled, but there was always very little mirth in the giggle of a French whore. It was like she was always plotting something. It was like she knew you knew, he thought, that you were being conned but the whole thing was a con, so why not enjoy? Little vixens with big dirty scheming minds. God love 'em.

There was just the right amount of soft yellow lamplight

to shadow the hard luck mileage on each of their faces, and make them look better than they really were—until a man got up close. It was a big room. Where the walls weren't mirrored, they shone slick in mahogany. Paintings of big-busted naked women hung from the walls. Whoever the artists were, Bad Zac didn't care; but he noted the women on the wall looked better in a creamy, sensuous kind of classical sense than the trollops in bed.

Fisting a cigar and his brass Zippo off a huge vanity dresser, Dillinger torched a fat stogie. Damn it! Something just didn't feel right.

"Man, this don't look good, not good at all, Bad One."

Dillinger turned, looked at Simms. "What?"

Johnny Simms whistled softly. "I've got less than a thousand francs on me."

Dillinger blew smoke. "Well, you got about nine hundred more than me, Johnny boy. A pity party, I ain't gonna throw for ya."

Simms whistled again, and the sound was starting to grate on Dillinger's nerves.

"Jesus," the black ex-merc went on, "y'know, we dipped into the team's war fund for this spree, Bad One, don't ya?"

"I know," Dillinger quietly growled. "Vic ain't gonna like it, but what's he gonna do? Shoot us?"

Simms whistled again, recounting his wad of francs to make sure he had the right little piddly figure.

"Jee-zus, the more I think about it, the worse it looks. Mister Vic tied up a lot of big paper in hardware and I'm starting to feel a little guilty about diving into those funds like there was gonna be no tomorrow, like we weren't gonna have to answer for it. The way I figure it, we spent about fifteen thousand American. Which means we'll owe about ten big ones when we get back."

"Don't sweat it, Johnny boy. And for the love of Christ, don't cry to me about debt either."

"Who's crying . . . now?"

"Listen, you wanna talk about debt. I got this head of white hair from what I called *shotgun* debt. I've owed half the fucking world money, and had the other half pissed off at me at the same time. I've been threatened, leaned on, pissed on and pissed off about owing and being owed. I know the score, here, so don't get all worked up. Vic won't get all shitty on us over fifteen lousy grand. We'll just have to pick up another assignment and pay it back. What are you gonna do anyway?" he asked and looked pointedly at the four whores. "Ask them to give it back?"

Brunette shook her mane. "No, no, no. You two are good, but not that good. And we will not start no tab with you, *monsieurs*. No credit. Francs first. Then play."

Dillinger cocked a grin at Simms. "See what I mean? And you thought they just plain old loved us."

Simms shoved the francs back into his pocket. "Just the same, I wouldn't mind recharging the battery and dive back in, Bad One."

Dillinger growled, "Do what you want. Piss on 'em, for all I care."

"Bay-bee. Why big ugly man so nasty to sweet leetle Mee-chell?"

Simms frowned. "What's the matter with you, man? You been standing by that window for the past ten minutes, walking all over your lip. What's eating you?"

Dillinger turned away from Simms, chomping on his cigar. He was starting to feel rude and ugly, didn't know exactly why he was getting so edgy.

"I dunno. My guts are getting all twisted up, Johnny boy. Something don't feel right."

"C'mon, Bad One. This ain't a Lauderdale strip joint. Don't go *deja vu* on me."

"More like *deja voodoo*, Johnny boy. Hey! Hey, you . . . what in the . . ."

Dillinger strode across the room. Brunette had unholstered one of his twin ivory-handled .45 Colts. Snatching the .45 out of her hand, he rasped, "That ain't no toy, wonder woman. I just had that ivory put on those butts. They were pearl before, so don't tell me your name's Pearl. 'Cause I ain't in the mood suddenly," he muttered to himself, holstering the .45.

"Lighten up, Bad One. Like you said, don't sweat Mister Vic's tab. It'll get taken care of."

"Yeah, like..."

Then Dillinger froze. He locked gazes with Simms. He pulled the cigar out of his mouth. With the crash of lightning and the peal of thunder, he couldn't be sure of what he heard at first. He sensed the tension from the whores.

Then he made out the sound. A steady burping sound. Someone was out in the hall with a goddamned silenced weapon.

A scream from beyond the door seemed to rip right through the walls.

Then, as if blasted off by gale force winds, the door exploded in a splinter of wood.

Dillinger and Simms were already moving as the room was flooded by a rolling tide of gunmen. Weapons blazed in the doorway, and figures charged into the whore's den.

2

If the situation hadn't been so deadly serious, it would have almost been comical. A grown man in his underwear in a room full of screaming drunken whores. Caught with his pants down, while only moments ago he had considered willing another hard-on . . . before mysterious gunmen came charging in the whore's den to make him limp forever.

There were certain things about life-threatening situations that Bad Zac Dillinger had learned from grim first-hand experience. Fear can be the most motivating or paralyzing force in a human being. Fear can damn near work miracles in a crisis. *Damn near.* Fear can speed up reaction time, and lightning reflexes can certainly shave the odds. Sometimes the odds can be too heavy. Sometimes more than sheer savagery and blinding speed are necessary. Things like luck—and maybe just a little divine intervention.

The invaders bulled into the room. Silenced subguns, which looked to Dillinger to be MAC-10s and mini-Uzis, were spitting out streams of lead. And waves of death. The big, white-haired ex-P.I. was a split second behind Johnny Simms. Together, they forged, like steel and lightning, into the flaming wall of lead. Only Dillinger discovered the lead was whistling right past him, nicking at earlobes and almost parting his scalp in the furious slipstream of tracking auto fire. Out of the corner of his eye, he saw a hellstorm of slugs chew up the red satin sheets. Piercing screams lanced the air. Brunette tumbled out of the bed. Dillinger found himself momentarily blinded by rage. All that lovely whoredom was being chopped up into something that resembled yesterday's digested hamburger meat. All that creamy, wanton, tainted flesh, never again to be lusted after, never again to be touched, except by the cold fingers of some cadaverous mortician doctoring the gruesome remains to make fit for a slightly less gruesome display.

A twisted pain ground up Dillinger's insides as if he'd swallowed broken glass. Pain, he had always believed, can also be one of the most motivating forces in a human being. A man who stacks up years of hard mileage, who has known, tasted, felt but conquered deep bitter pain can become one of the most dangerous creatures on the face of the earth if he's backed into a corner, if that pain suddenly comes bursting to the surface out of nowhere and for whatever reason.

Primed to kick the last bit of ass he ever would on earth, Zac Dillinger knew he was going to be checking out in a matter of eyeblinks. And he would be heading out, together with Johnny Simms, one of the only three real friends he had in the whole stinking world. As Dillinger craned a hook kick off an invader's jaw, he glimpsed Simms, a fifth-degree black belt, going to work with the deadly precision of some concentration camp doctor. A gut shot, a nut shot and a head butt, and three guys were sprawling all over the carpet, regretting the day they'd slithered into the world from their momma's womb. Simms grabbed a fourth killer, dropped on his back. Foot plunging into the guy's breadbasket, Simms rolled backwards. A body was launched across the room, where it crashed into the vanity dresser. Shards tumbled around that guy, but he leapt up, bellowing with rage.

A left and a right, and Dillinger sent two more goons reeling away. A hollow ringing in Dillinger's ears, and something told him he was being cracked in the head with fists or machine gun butts. It didn't matter. He was the charging bull, looking to gore any and all comers. He was so pumped up with adrenaline that he didn't even realize the invaders had stopped triggering their weapons.

More gun-wielding invaders surged into the room. A backhand hammerfist and a reverse spinning kick from Simms, and two more victims had their lights punched out. Bodies slammed into mirrors, shattering more glass.

But the force of added numbers quickly crushed in on Dillinger and Simms, and hemmed them inside a wall of thudding flesh. The invaders began using their subguns like baseball bats. A fist rocketed into the side of Simms's face, driving him back toward the pool of blood and naked twitching flesh on the bed.

Light suddenly supernovaed in Dillinger's eyes. He bulled through the swinging subguns, clipped another guy on the jaw with a short chopping right that snapped his enemy's head sideways. More lights exploded in Dillinger's sight. A terrible ringing split his skull. Nausea bubbled into his throat. Two more slashing blows to his head, and he tasted the blood filling his mouth. Then his legs seemed to turn to rubber. As he dropped, he saw Simms pummeled about the face and head by about a half-dozen goons. Finally, the black ex-merc was utterly still. Dillinger thought he heard his friend groan, but he couldn't be sure. He struggled through the roaring in his ears to sit up, but a boot drilled into his ribs, gutted the wind out of him. He felt as if he was teetering on the edge of some precipice, fighting desperately to remain conscious. Through a haze, he looked around the room.

The horror, he saw, had only begun.

The invaders began tearing the room apart. One of the whores, Dillinger saw, was still alive. It was the brunette, Paulette, Dillinger thought her name was. Another goon ripped the wad of francs out of Simms's pants pocket, then kicked the black ex-merc in the face and laughed. Drawers were tossed across the room, and more francs were pocketed. A simple fucking robbery? Dillinger thought. No. It can't be. There had to more to it than that.

Two of the goons took turns raping the brunette. Her whimpering sounds of fear and cries of pain seemed to reach Dillinger's ears from a mile away. It was like something out of the Dark Ages, Dillinger thought, as if the Goths had ridden into town and all the nubile wenches were up for grabs. He looked toward the doorway. Strips of wood hung down, but he could clearly see the madness just beyond the shattered door. There was a naked whore out in the hallway, and she was on her knees, making strangled little sounds, tears streaming down her face. There was a shadow, standing in front of the woman. Through the crimson mist, Dillinger watched, as the shadow zipped up his pants, then, without hesitation, put a snub little pistol to her temple and squeezed the trigger. Christ, Dillinger thought, what is this insanity?

He started to roll up on his side, then he saw another tall shadow slide through the door, slapping at the jagged shards as if they were bugs buzzing around his face. And it was a face unlike any Dillinger had ever seen. A face that looked dead even in life. Gray eyes that had seen every horror and suffering the world could throw up, eyes that were piercing at that very moment, it seemed, right into his soul, measuring the amount of horror and suffering that he himself had endured and judging whether or not he was worthy to join the ranks of the damned. The face looked like it was carved out of stone, a long, gaunt face, a death's head for goddamn sure. There was a hideous white scar on that face, and Zac Dillinger had the grim feeling he was staring up the face of Death itself. The scar just stared down at him.

"You're in luck."

Luck? Dillinger looked up at the scar. He hurt so bad, he had the twisted desire suddenly to just laugh, but the feeling blocked up somewhere deep in his belly. He was in a world of trouble, he knew, for he was clinging to the edge of the judgment seat by the skin of his fingernails. But he knew he wouldn't let his character die in humiliation at this moment of judgment. No, he wasn't the kind of man to beg for his life, nor would Johnny Simms dare even dream of clinging onto to the last sniveling snot of hope. When it came down to the end, and Dillinger knew the end was upon him and Johnny Simms, they'd go out like they had lived. Like lions. But even lions can be dropped by some lily-livered chickenshit with a hi-powered rifle, and made to lay in their own blood while the hunter gloats and thumps his chest. Like he's really done something.

And the hunters were definitely gloating in the whore's den.

"I've decided to spare you and your black friend."

The voice seemed to drift down on Dillinger. A cold voice. A dead voice full of dead things.

Dillinger sensed some kind of uneasy stillness in the room right then. His ears rang. Thunder seemed to crash down on the cathouse from just a few feet above. The crackle of lightning tore through his pounding head. He spat a gummy ball of blood on the carpet. There was a tooth, staring up at him like some obscene thing, bogged down in the slick wad of his life's juices.

"You see, it's not just you and your black friend we want," the voice called down, all steel, all judgment. "You're merely tools. You're merely nothing in the Big Scheme. Besides, there are many sides to everything, and all is not what it appears to be. Reality can often seem unreal, and unreality can often be quite real. You see, I want you to know that I can be a man of mercy. And I want you to know that I have experienced some real personal growth in this room tonight."

Dillinger felt his head spinning. Blackness began to waver in his eyes. *What the fuck are you talking about, jack? Personal growth? Let me grow my foot about a yard up your ass until I can drive your guts right out your mouth.*

Dillinger heard the whimpering. He saw Paulette's terrified face, a contorted hazy mask in his eyes. The scar pulled something out of his trenchcoat. No, Dillinger heard his mind scream. Enough, he wanted to say, but the word seemed locked up in the bile churning in his belly.

The scar unscrewed the silencer off the pistol. He put the pistol to Paulette's temple. There was a crack, a piercing sound that drove a spike through Dillinger's brain. The world seemed to fall away from Zac Dillinger. He let himself fall, hard and fast into the blackness. He took her face down into the blackness with him, and he wanted to cry for her. Cry for the insanity that he'd witnessed. Cry for Johnny Simms. But the blackness consumed him almost instantly, and sent him plunging into some dark pool of fear and pain and hate.

ALL ACTION! ALL GUTS!
Don't miss any of the exciting books in
Dan Schmidt's EAGLE FORCE SERIES:

Action on Eighteen Wheels!

Marc Lee and Carl Browne, ex-Delta Force anti-terrorist commandos: They've taken on bloodthirsty Middle Eastern terrorists...deadly drug cartels...vicious bikers...the Mafia...no matter how badly they're outnumbered, Lee and Browne always come up swinging...and blasting!

Don't miss any of the exciting books in Bob Ham's OVERLOAD SERIES!